CONTENTS

Part Three: *Inheriting the Earth*

Part Four: *Tired of Waiting for Home*

Introduction by Mark Budman

HUMAN MIGRATION BEGAN at the dawn of humanity, but immigration is a much newer phenomenon. To have immigration, you need countries with defined borders, people willing and able to cross them, and other people whose jobs are to prevent their crossing. The more prosperous (or more paranoid) the country is, the more difficult it is to cross its borders—and the more difficult it will be to stay in that country once you cross said borders.

In the eyes of natives, immigration is either a tool to enhance the country's prosperity, and its social and moral standing, or the scourge that undermines the country's economical and ethical foundation. Immigration is the reason for some of the most profound and often violent and deadly discourse that the United States and most Western countries are facing today.

As a first-generation émigré from the former USSR, I know the plight and accomplishments of my fellow immigrants first-hand. But one thing is clear even for everyone, whichever side they favor: immigrants are more mobile and dynamic than most people with longer roots, and this mobility requires both determination and stamina. Immigrant writers possess both of these qualities in excess.

We invited first- and second-generation immigrants to contribute their short stories (1000 words or fewer) to increase our readers' understanding of immigration discourse through the power of fiction.

In the process of selection, we didn't take any political sides and we chose the stories according to their literary merits and the spirit of the anthology. The stories and their authors came from all over the world. Their homelands are Vietnam, Morocco, India, Ukraine, Germany, Canada, Israel, the UK, Romania, China, Moldova, Cuba, Poland, South Africa, and of course, the USA.

The forty stories of our anthology are not designed to change or reinforce your existing opinions on immigration and immigrants. They are open windows into different worlds, windows you might have missed before you took this slim book into your hands. Believe in the most powerful—though not necessarily violent—force of the human world: the written word. Give the word a chance.

PART ONE

Past the limits of the familiar

The Immigrant Leaves, Again by Shaun Levin

THAT'S ME WAVING from the back of the boat as we leave the shore that did not welcome and did not expel. We expected nothing less. Watch me untangle myself from the past twenty years as I unravel away from the island. Have we said enough goodbyes? Those are the chimneys and the rooftops. Bye-bye, chimneys. The novelty of a chimney—a *chimney*—after so many lands lived in and then we arrive, clamouring for shore. Hello, island. That's me emerging from the water like the fish they say begat us. This is from whence you came, fish in the sea, the offspring of those who dared to walk, who could no longer suffer the water. Travel back far enough and you'll see our ancestors, fish on dry land. Hello, shore; hello, rocks; hello, sand. Hello, island. Oh my God, you cannot imagine the languages I've been through to get here—a Velcro of tongues, maneuvering my way through crowded markets and the back streets of shopping malls. Say that in Xhosa. Say it in Russian. Say something in your language. Which one exactly? Now it's goodbye, English (language). Goodbye, English (people). There's a limit, too. There's a limit. Honestly. Bye-bye, island. I'm off. I admit there are days when I miss those chimneys and bridges, I do, the straight lines of your existence. This is how I came to you on my belly—a serpent out of Eden, terrible things witnessed, so close to the action. We're all witnesses [hello, English (people)] no matter how isolated, no matter how jagged the rocks of our shorelines. We all stand in the concentric circles of immorality. Do you mean immortality? Watch us pull away from the shore. Goodbye, shore; goodbye, island. Who knows what language we'll land up in next? Thanks for coming to wave us goodbye before heading back to your sofas where the wood crackles behind the grate and smoke rises—hello chimneys—to cover your cities in a veil of... What? It's hard to see from so far away. This is me extracting myself. Floppy disk from hard-drive, video cassette from player. I have it all on record. I arrived with nothing and now I leave with a memory stick under my armpit. It's cold here in the middle of darkness as we huddle closer. There's nothing warmer than this cod-spawn of proximity, eyes growing bigger as we adjust to the light, reaching for something beyond the haze and nothingness of the fog on your shore. So we turn our heads from it and face the whatever it is that is before us, a new land on which to hatch.

A Nice Boy by Raffi Boyadjian

"OH, DEAR!"

A tall, thin man crashed into me in the crowded airport, spilling me and my comic books across the floor. My chin throbbed from smashing it on the ground.

"Are you OK, son?"

I didn't understand a word as he lifted me off the floor and picked up my books. His voice had a lilt, like a glissando. I liked the sound but stood there silently, noticing moist blue eyes under arched eyebrows. He reminded me of Opa. I already missed him. I missed everyone.

"Are you OK?"

He kept standing there. I began worrying that he was angry, though his expression belied that. I dared not rub my chin, lest it set him off. He noticed my comic books weren't English.

He pointed at me. "*Dootch*?"

I nodded. My mother returned from the carousel with our suitcases. I ran to her as he handed over my things, apologizing.

"I knocked your son over. I'm very sorry."

My mother answered in halting English. "He iz OK."

The man pulled a dollar out of his pocket and crouched down to hand it to me. I looked at the strange bill.

"Zay sank you."

I looked at her, not understanding the instruction.

"*Sag danke*."

"*Danke*."

He patted my head, then rushed off.

I rubbed my chin as I examined the bill. It was green and white and warm. I held it against my cheek. It smelled musty. My mother grabbed the suitcases and headed down the corridor to join my father, brother, and sister in the customs office.

"*Komm schon, kindchen*."

I ran to keep pace.

We entered a small office. A small aluminum tree with blinking, colored lights sat atop a grey file cabinet. Two red paper bells in opposite corners and a gold garland connecting them framed an otherwise bare wall. Hardly cheery. The man talking to my father reminded me of the bald sidekick in *The Great Race*. I watched it with my uncles and aunts in Höchst the week before we left. I laughed until tears rolled. Especially during the pie-throwing scene. My father motioned to my mother.

"Heer ees."

My mother took over signing paperwork, while my father dealt with my fidgeting infant sister who'd just awoken and began crying. My brother stood next to his chair with his arms wrapped around my father's leg.

"What is the nature of your visit?"

"Ve arr nut visiteeng. Ve arr leeveeng heer."

"You're leaving?"

"No. Ve arr komming heer."

"You're returning from a trip?"

"*Ach*... Ve hov movet heer."

"You're moving here?"

"*Ja*!"

"Customs gave me the wrong information." He ripped up the forms my mother had been signing and pulled new ones out of his desk. My father frowned.

"*Was ist loss?*"

She shushed him.

"Do you have your visas?"

"Yes." She handed them over.

He held up my mother's and father's visas while checking their faces against the pictures. "This man is your husband?"

"Yes."

"How long have you been married?"

"Ayt yeaz."

He bent forward to fill in the forms. The blonde fuzz on top of his head looked like the fuzz on my sister's head.

"These are your children?"

"Yes."

He held up our visas to match our faces. "How old are they?"

"Von, feif und zex yeaz oold."

He winked at me as he handed the visas back. I clutched my comics close to my chest. My mother stroked my hair and whispered that I should tell the man what she taught me. I shook my head.

"*Bitte.*"

"I EM eh NAYSE BOYee." My cheeks burned. My mother beamed at her polyglot son.

"I'm sure you are, kid." He handed me a candy from the same drawer where he'd gotten the forms. I put it in my mouth, then spat it out. Butterscotch. What a cruel trick.

My father smacked my head.

My head hurt. Not merely from the smack, or the fall. The unfamiliarity of everything—the bright lights made my temples throb, my eyes burn. The cacophony of beeping trams and rolling luggage and rushing travelers and staccato announcements over intercoms... I hated it here. I missed my uncles and aunts and Oma and Opa. I missed my friends. How was I going to make friends here when I couldn't understand anyone? Everybody talked like they were chewing gum. *Ngow, ngow*... I bit my lip to keep from crying. I failed. Which set my sister off again. Which angered my father. My mother snatched my sister from him and sealed our fate with a flourish of her wrist. She slid the forms over to my father to countersign.

It was then, with those signatures, that I realized that my parents wouldn't look out for me. The packing, the goodbyes, even the flight—it all seemed reversible, but this action was indelible. This epiphany made me sob. My brother joined in, making it a trio.

"*Verdammt noch mal!*" My father picked up my brother and yanked me hard, toward the door.

My mother apologized to the man as he handed back our visas. "Dey arr verry teyered."

He nodded.

The door closed behind us. My father, brother, and I stood in the bright hallway. I could still hear my sister's crying over my own. My father jerked my arm and glowered down at me. I stopped crying immediately, though my shoulders still convulsed.

"*Halt's maul!*"

My brother stopped as well, knowing it was prudent. My father sighed angrily and lit a cigarette. It dangled between his lips as he ran his hands through his hair.

The cigarette burned to the filter before the door opened and my mother came out with my sister. She'd stopped crying and was sucking her thumb.

"Welcome to the United States."

"Sank you verry match."

"*Fertig?*"

My mother handed him the paperwork along with my sister, ignoring his question. She picked up my brother. I took her hand as we headed down the long hallway toward our connecting flight. I looked up at her as a tear hit my forehead.

Unexpected Sunday Meeting by Lazar Trubman

GORGEOUS MORNING IN the awakened city: fresh new green, the angled rays of the sun glittering in spiders' webs, birds twittering, the fragrance of buds, grass drenched in dew, the air cool, bees hovering around blossoming branches, Sunday, the tolling of a distant bell... Spring in Chisinau!

It had been months since Florin was liberated from the Colony of Strict Regime in Northern Russia. Behind him were dozens of blood transfusions, restorative dental tortures, and scary talks with a cardiologist. He had obtained his so-so bill of health and was waiting patiently for the Soviet Immigration Office to approve his visa.

One day, as he was sipping coffee at a small table outside of a restaurant in downtown Chisinau, a hand lightly touched his shoulder:

"What are you up to these days, Florin, what are you up to?"

The voice sounded unfamiliar, as well as the short laugh that followed. Florin turned around to see the man.

At first, he didn't recognize Professor Luca Oliescu as he stood there in front of him. It wasn't just his voice, but his face; pale and utterly different. And yet Florin still felt that he knew him. Something in his aspect could never be changed.

"Don't you remember me?" asked Luca, noticing Florin's confusion. "Yes, yes, they can do this to you—they and their newly invented millstones! But your Colony wasn't a vacation either, I've been told."

Florin kept looking at Luca's face in silence. In reality, it was no longer a face, but two cheekbones with thin skin over them, sticking out like miniature mountain peaks, and the muscles—which formed an expression that reminded him of Professor Oliescu—were so weak that they couldn't hold his laugh for a long time. That's why his laugh was short and much too large; it distorted his face, which seemed huge in relation to his eyes, which were set far back in his skull.

"Professor!" exclaimed Florin, stopping himself from adding, *I was told that you were dead!* Instead, he asked, "Well, well, how the hell are you?"

"I'm great, Florin, I'm great!" Luca put up another short laugh. "It's spring in Chisinau, nature's booming awakening!"

Florin tried to understand why he kept laughing. He knew Luca as a serious man, as Professor of Electromagnetics at the Chisinau State University, but every time he opened his mouth, his face formed that uncanny expression of mirth. To ask seemed impossible.

"Those millstones roughed me up quite a bit," said Luca. "But I got lucky." He paused, and Florin had a chance to study him. Actually, he wasn't laughing at all, any more than two cheekbones with skin over them could laugh. Florin apologized for not recognizing him at first.

"You're not alone, my friend," assured Luca, "but I've gotten used to it."

"I'm sorry," Florin said again. "I feel embarrassed." He felt an impulse to leave, to tell Luca about the conference—the real reason for his trip to Chisinau—but before he could speak, Luca began coughing and couldn't stop, and when he finally did, Florin saw two bloody spots percolating through his handkerchief.

"Scary, isn't it?" said Luca. "But not as scary as a few other things I'm hiding under my clothes."

"We all have our scars to show, I guess," said Florin. "Some deeper than others."

"Don't we, colleague? Scars of the century, aren't they?"

His skin looked as if it could crack at any moment, like old leather or clay, and he had a belly that looked like a small party balloon suspended under his thin ribs. His eyes were the only thing unchanged since Florin last saw him—lovely, but sunken. He glanced at his wristwatch.

"Why are you suddenly in such a hurry?" asked Luca. "How about a drink for the occasion?"

He had been Florin's colleague back in the old days at the university. Florin looked up to him and respected him more than any other professor in the country, but he really had no time for a drink. "My dear professor," he said, because Luca was holding him by the arm, "I do have to go. My conference starts in less than an hour."

"Then some other time, right?" said Luca, and Florin knew in that moment that this man was really already dead.

"Yes, I should like that," he said, paying for his coffee. "Whenever I'm in Chisinau again."

Maybe it *was* a laugh, he thought, while checking the street for a taxi. Maybe Luca kept laughing all the time because he was still alive, standing in front of him in downtown Chisinau, despite the rumors that he had been badly tortured and died in the camp.

As luck would have it, a taxi stopped next to them, and a young couple paid and got out. Florin slipped into the back seat, lowered the window, and said, "It was nice to see you alive and laughing—"

"We should meet again, Florin!" interrupted Luca. "I have a lot to tell you—enough for a thick book—and I hope you're still a good listener."

"I'm always up for a good story, Professor," said Florin. "Always up for a good story."

He tried to distinguish the color of Luca's eyes and couldn't.

"In the meantime, call me," said Luca, stepping back from the taxi. "It is allowed now."

"I will," promised Florin, and he gave the driver a sign to go.

"You may take a nap," said the driver moving into the traffic. "It's quite a ride."

"Can you make it in thirty minutes?"

"I'll certainly try."

"You'll be rewarded," promised Florin. We're damaged goods, he thought, cranking up the window and closing his eyes. But it's rubbish that we are dying; we're just getting awfully tired and more often than not need bypasses, transplants, dentures, and blood transfusions. And when none of that helps, when we run out of the last ounce of strength, we move aside. In silence.

On the Counter by Yara Zgheib

DOCUMENTS FANNED OUT on the counter like a hand of poker, and not a good one. Not the good side of the partition to be standing on, either. The agent glances at them, unimpressed. I attempt disinterest and fail. My forehead hits the glass—too well-cleaned. I had not noticed I was leaning.

My passport is blue and not good, either. An accident of birth whose pages—labeled, packaged—have since followed me around, weighing in on my life choices. I glare at the booklet, resentful and overcome with self-pity. *If only*... thought every person who, by one digit, ever lost the lottery.

Passe. Port. Un passeport, historically, was a note that gave its owner the freedom to go past the limits of the kingdom. Past the limits of the familiar, to travel safely across foreign lands and seas into foreign ports that then stopped being so foreign.

Pass. Port. A passport, eventually, became a leatherbound record of a gentleman's agreement between the leaders of nations: "I will respect and protect your citizens. You will do the same for mine." Implied: a universal recognition of the freedom of movement.

"Your passport please."

I place it on the counter. Who knows, today, what it means.

Feet starting to ache, I shift my weight around. The agent does not look up. The agent could not care less; she has never stood, will never stand, on this side of the counter.

She will never have to; she rolled a hard six. I wonder, though, at which point in her own family lineage another immigrant must have stood. At which point and at what counter had someone raised eyes like hers, hopes like mine? I think of the twelve million someones who landed in the port on Ellis Island.

The "tired, poor, huddled masses yearning to breathe, the wretched refuse of teeming shores. The homeless, tempest-tost." I wonder: Did they find safe harbor here? Would they still, if they were standing here today? Would their passports be deemed worthy of a stamp? Mine is retained by the agent.

I am told to return to the waiting room. My former seat has been taken; there are at least one hundred other people here. Each, like me, has a number. As do the counters behind which our applications are being read. Seven of them reviewing, mechanically, who knows how many of us. This number system is septic, I observe.

As is the silence in the room. All eyes are raised toward the blinking screens calling the hopefuls one at a time to counters for their passports and verdicts. My four digits flash next to Counter 5. Purse, folder, heart in my hand, I scramble over. The agent—a different one this time, but with same face—has my answer, and it's not a good one.

I walk away from the counter. I can. There is freedom in that, too. A chosen one. Outside, I exhale. Inside, others are still waiting.

Fishing for a New Life by Marina Villa

THE SEA LOOKED calmer today, so he approached the pier with a fishing pole in hand and walked up to the man reading the newspaper under a canopy.

"Can I take one of your fishing boats out for the day?"

The man stood up and said, "Comrade, you've come too late. All the good boats are already out, and these are reserved."

"How about that one?" Omar pointed to a small rowboat vigorously wobbling from side to side.

"Oh, well, you can take that one, but I would not go far. Beware that if the wind picks up, you might capsize."

"I'll take it."

From under the canopy, the man shook his head and grinned as he watched Omar throw his fishing pole inside the boat and clumsily climb in. Not even a water jug. He could tell Omar was no fisherman; his lily-white skin denoted a life of comfort, free from physical drudgery. Yup, this was no fisherman. Others had tried before, and they returned an hour or two later, exhausted, with skin sizzling from the sun.

Omar struggled to maneuver the boat away, and after an hour of vigorously rowing against the current, he reached the fishing waters, which—from the pier—had only looked a stone's-throw away. His hands were starting to blister, but he continued to row past the fishing boats, heading north.

He knew now that the journey would take longer than he had expected. He realized, too, that his plan to row for one hour and rest for a half-hour was unrealistic since he had not taken the current into account, which pulled him back every time he stopped.

Still, he continued.

Two days later he lay at the bottom of the boat in the open sea, drifting in and out of consciousness. When he could summon the strength, he lifted his head and watched shapes move below the water, spirits from another world. He longed for the soothing cover of night, for darkness to alleviate his pain, to help him forget, but scenes from his life jolted him back to consciousness with unrelenting sharpness.

He shook his head from side to side to dispel the looping replay of that one moment—two years ago—when he walked out on his two young daughters and their mother. Their faces, sad and confused, gradually turned bitter and condemning with each reenactment.

He coughed to moisten his throat, but his body—mistreated and neglected as so many other essentials in his life—refused to cooperate.

Visions of his mother floated past. Her love and kindness calmed the shivers that wracked him despite the intensity of the sun. Yet he had walked out on her for reasons he only now understood. He relived all the times she had paid his gambling debts, the times she opened her door when he—suitcase in hand—showed up after another failed romance.

Now he realized that her presence suffocated him. Her eyes, those mirrors for his many flaws, were too painful to bear. Each one of her wrinkles lay witness to his countless failures.

He took some comfort in knowing that she will be the one—perhaps the only one—who will notice his absence.

A gust of wind caressed his body, offering him a moment of relief, and his mind shifted from his mother to his entanglement with the underground in support of the doomed US-led Bay of Pigs Invasion. For once he had embraced a noble cause, made an effort to redeem himself—but this, too, ended in failure. Now the militia was going house-to-house in search of conspirators. With some delight, he envisioned the moment in which his daughters will hear about the arsenal found in his apartment. They will at least know that his outspoken support for the Revolution was a cover-up. They might even consider him a hero.

A dreadful thought invaded: What if his actions put them in danger?

No, not possible. He had left them long before his involvement with the underground. With this, his torment subsided, and he passed out.

When his senses stirred again, he could no longer feel the rhythmic motion of the sea, but pain assured him that he was still alive.

Beeping sounds and hushed voices surrounded him. He opened his eyes, and squinted, blinded by fluorescent lights, chalk-white walls and ceiling. His body was covered in gauze. A woman—a nurse?—oddly cheerful and energetic, asked him a question that he could not understand. She shrugged at his confusion and fiddled with a contraption connected to his arm.

A man approached his bedside.

"*Como te sientes?*"

Ah. He curved his cracked lips into a faint smile and answered in his native Spanish. "Could be better. Where am I?"

"Mercy Hospital in Miami. The US Coast Guard found you. They thought you were dead, but once they had you on board, they detected a trace of life and brought you here.

You are one of the lucky ones." He bent over the bed so Omar could see him better. "I'm Paco Hernández. And you are…"

"Omar Rodríguez." His fingers moved in a failed attempt to offer a handshake.

"Omar, I'm here to help you. We Cubans take care of each other. Once you are released from the hospital, I will find you a place to stay and I will help you find a job." Then he added, "Do you know anyone?"

"No."

Paco's face blurred, and he closed his eyes. But as he faded, he heard a whisper, "We will talk more when you are feeling better."

No—he forced himself awake. "I need your help now… my mother…please let her know that I'm alright…"

He saw Paco nod.

"One more thing…my daughters…their mother…I need to get them out."

He did not hear a response, but he felt the warmth of Paco's hand on his, and this was all he needed before falling into a deep and peaceful sleep.

Raft by Philip Charter

A LARGE AFRICAN man looks around the office. It is stripped bare apart from a table and chairs. Even seated, he is nearly a head taller than the man with a uniform and a name badge—Juan. The two men look at each other across the table, through the silent steam of the teapot.

Juan inspects his fingernails and weighs his first move.

"Do you need a translator?"

"No. I speak your language."

Juan removes a damaged photo from a plastic wallet. "Can you tell me about this?"

The man remains silent, his features muted. He reaches for the photograph, then changes his mind.

"We need to identify them. Do they have documents?" asks Juan.

"No documents. I cannot help you."

"We can speed up your application."

The man bows his head and begins to cry. Juan busies himself pouring the teas.

"That's me in the middle," the man says between sobs. "The whole village is there." He swallows. "Now only me."

It's only been one day since the crossing from Libya. The hours huddling together felt like years, clinging to the raft as it was tossed about like a cheap paper plate.

"And who was with you?"

"Son, daughter, and my brother's family. My wife stay at home." A tear rolls down the man's pudgy cheek and narrowly misses the paper photograph. "You cannot tell her. You must not—"

"Can you write the names for me?"

The man writes the names.

Juan reaches across the table and rests his hand on the man's for a second, then takes the paper.

After a pause, Juan speaks. "We want to reduce the deaths."

The man looks up, through watery eyes. He shakes his head.

"Who did you pay?"

"I cannot."

"Think of what you came for. A better life," says Juan, smiling.

The man is not listening. "I tried to drown, but my body don't let me."

"Who put you on the boat?"

"They kill me." He draws a finger across his throat.

"Anything you can tell us. The payment, the dates, any faces you remember…"

The man shakes his head again.

Juan sighs and takes out a packet of cigarettes. "We need to keep the photo, for identification. I'm sorry." He slides the photo back toward the plastic wallet.

"No." The man catches his hand and stops him.

"You'll regret it if you don't tell me now," says Juan. "There is no more time."

"What does time matter to me? You people will still be asking the same questions in a hundred years."

The tea sits between the two men, untouched.

Tasting Life by Jose Varghese

There are a lot of notices pinned to the big tent's outer wall. The hands of the man smell of tobacco. His hairy forearm brushes past my ears as he gently pushes me forward by my neck. The hem of his coat rubs my left shoulder. I miss Baba. Baba's arms aren't hairy or greasy, and he never smokes. I miss Mama, too. I miss the baklava she made when all three of us were home for the last time. I wish I didn't have to miss them and everything about home.

The weight of the hand lifts once we're inside. There are four corners, and it looks almost like a room. I face three tables; each has a man in formal clothing sitting behind it on a plastic chair. I turn back for a clue, but the hairy arm's owner is gone. I didn't understand what he whispered to the men before going away.

One of them motions me to sit on the stool in front of his table. He speaks in a language that everyone speaks here. A language that makes no sense to me. He smiles at me and offers a cheese triangle from a round box. It is cold, as if taken directly from the fridge. I feel tears burn my cheeks as I take a bite greedily, hoping to taste a trace of Mama's baklava in it. The men talk to one another in hushed tones. I assume it's about me. Maybe they are saying how hungry I seem. I don't care. It's been two long days since I've eaten anything or drunk proper water—the kind that doesn't taste funny.

The man motions me to stand up and look at a camera. He offers me a tissue to wipe the stains of cheese off my lips before the camera clicks. I wish someone had given me a full meal. I know I can't complain because this is the end—or beginning—of a journey. And I know that things won't be the same again.

I am made to sit down again, as the man jots something down on several papers. He holds in his left hand my passport and a few other papers the hairy-arms-man had given him. He keeps them at a distance and squints at them through his thick glasses whenever he has to fill a new entry. He says something to the others, and they all stare at me, trying to make it look as if they aren't really staring at me.

I feel like crying, but I stay strong. I bite my lower lip hard, in a deliberate attempt to hurt myself. It's a good distraction. I taste blood where I bit my lip. I like it, so I suck in and swallow it. I try not to look at the men.

There is an air cooler in the middle of the tent. It rotates and sends a chilly breeze in all directions. I fight the temptation to place my palms in front of it and feel it closer. I remember the days on which I would stand naked in front of the AC in my room, right out of a shower, hoping to catch a cold so that I could have an excuse for a day or two off from school.

The man smiles and hands me a big folder file that weighs a ton. He motions me to move to the next table. It takes effort to walk and I trip over the cooler's wire. The second man stands up, comes running, lifts me up, and steadies me. He takes the file and its papers that have scattered on the floor and walks me to his table.

The third man says something and goes out. He comes back with the hairy-armed man, who holds a brown paper packet that smells of food. He places it on the table in front of me. My mouth waters despite the bad memories that keep rushing back.

As they begin to open the food packet, my vision blurs. The aroma wafts in and out. I close my eyes and try to push away the memory of how perfect our house looked and smelled on the day everything changed. Home. Baba. Mama. Mere memories now.

I sense two of the men standing behind me, one holding my shoulders and speaking to me, as everything around me begins to shake and go up and down in large circles. A heaviness claims my head. I try to sit still to avoid falling down.

I get water. I drink it. The hunger comes back. The smells too. Sweat. Cooked lentils. Tobacco. Fresh bread. Hummus. Pickle.

He breaks the bread, dips it in the lentil dish, and begins to feed me. It tastes great. I try to smile at him.

Hairy arm. Tobacco smell.

Crossing the Line by James Corpora

"*La Migra*..." THE coyote said, glancing around as if he were looking for the Border Patrol. His mouth was open, and he seemed to pant slightly even though it was a cool night. His tongue lolled over the tops of his teeth, dripping saliva.

"*La Migra* has eyes that see in the night, and machines that go everywhere. You cannot escape him."

The coyote had asked for two hundred and fifty dollars to lead them across, and he watched closely as he waited for their response to his offer.

"Is it difficult to cross here?" Ramón asked.

"Difficult? There are a thousand ways to cross, and a thousand paths, but only I know the one true path. Most cross over there." He nodded in a direction that looked as if it led nowhere.

"*Doscientos dólares?*" Ramón asked.

Berto's father was shrewd—a hard bargainer in Mexico, but this was different.

"No," the coyote replied. "*Dos cinquenta.*"

"*Pues, dos veinte.*"

"*Bueno. Dos veinte.* You see, you have already bargained me down thirty dollars."

The coyote's eyes became small and red. He spat.

"Two hundred dollars will not get you that far."

Both looked in the direction of the tiny ball of spit. It

was the path, maybe. But no, the coyote looked in another direction now.

"How much money do you have?" he said to the boy standing next to Ramón.

Berto turned out one pants pocket and then the other. He removed the hat from his head and showed the coyote the inside. The money was in his shoe, the left one.

The coyote grunted. "I should strip you. It is in your sock maybe."

He took his revolver then and held the barrel next to Berto's left eye. Berto could feel it there, cold and hard, with a bullet nestling in one of the chambers.

"Give me your money," the coyote said. "All of it."

Berto made a gesture with his hands, first turning them palms up and then flipping them over.

The coyote nudged him with the revolver so that the pressure on the outside of his eyeball was about equal to the pressure inside. A little more and his eyeball would rupture. He cocked the gun. The chamber turned and crystals tumbled as Berto waited for it to explode.

"*Uno...*" the coyote said. "I am counting. You have until three."

"Leave him alone," Ramón said.

He reached into his pocket and pulled out several bills. Berto was surprised; he didn't know his father had that much money.

"A hundred dollars," Ramón said to the coyote. "Take it."

The coyote hesitated. He pressed the barrel of the revolver a little harder to Berto's eye, and for an instant Berto didn't think he would make it. There would be a blast and the bullet would tear through his eye, bone, brain, and go out through the back of his head. They would not cross that night and he would not see his home again, for the United

States was his home, not Mexico. He had lived his entire life in the United States.

"No one will take you for a hundred dollars," the coyote said. "Not here, not anywhere. Not even in *Tejas*."

"I know," Ramón said, pushing the money in the coyote's direction. "But you are very fair. Here, take this. It is yours."

The gun finally came down and Berto felt his eye spring back. It pulsed, and it was red now, but it was his and it was whole.

"To the head of the path only," the coyote said. "I will not take you across. You will have to cross on your own. A hundred dollars... I would not risk my life for that." He pocketed the money.

"But is it a good path?"

"Yes, it is an excellent path, and it will get you across. But keep to your left, and pay no attention to what others are doing. You will find many chickens inside—some running here, others there—and each group with a coyote at its head. Let them go their own way. Once you reach the other side you will be all right. At this hour it should be safe. No patrols."

The coyote left them at the head of a path, saying nothing to them. He simply disappeared.

They plunged in, letting the path lead them down through brush and then up the canyon on the far side. They heard sounds, sensed others, but saw no one. Once, there was a scurrying in some nearby bushes, but Ramón pushed on. A second time they heard someone moan.

"What is it?" Ramón asked in a hoarse whisper.

"I don't know, papa."

"*Espérame aquí.*" And he disappeared into the bushes.

Berto heard the second man speak again; there was the sound of scuffling, then silence. He waited. There was a small stabbing sound and a breath of air on his cheek as if it had come from the depths of someone's soul. Minutes passed. Then Ramón suddenly reappeared from out of the darkness.

"Nothing," he said. "Only the coyote."

There were lights ahead of them now and stars above. No moon, but the stars and lights seemed to go on forever.

"Look," Ramón replied. "It is America."

But Berto's eyes were on his father now, and it was as if he was seeing him for the first time. Suddenly he knew what had happened in the darkness behind them. He knew the stabbing sound and the breath of air on his cheek.

"Papa..." he said.

"I had to..." Ramón replied. "He wanted more money. He was a thief. Worth nothing."

Berto's eyes went wide and dark, as wide as he could make them, as if to let in all the light he could. To see all he could. Understand all. He wanted to say something to Ramón, a word. Anything. But he couldn't.

Joseph and his Brothers by Alizah Teitelbaum

ONCE THERE WAS a child named Joseph. Before he was born, his mother and father lived in America. Someone had stolen their other children, and his mother screamed and yelled, and in the womb, Joseph acquired passion, guilt, rage, and heartache. Random sparks entered his brain and exploded as a prayer, which hurt the robbers, and his parents got their kids back. They sued for enough money to move to Israel by the time Joseph got his first haircut at age three.

However, nothing worked over there.

People said Joseph would grow up better if he didn't listen to his parents' impure American speech at the *Shabbat* table.

Joseph's mother tried to steer the conversation to holy subjects, but it was so easy to slip.

It started with an innocent comment:

It was so hot, and now it's cold.

This reminded Father of a very cold winter in Brooklyn, when his old buddy Zulu used to stage confrontations, like beating up policemen. But Zulu gave it up since nobody helped him besides junkies and derelicts.

Mother shot Father a look, so he changed the subject to his graduation trip in Europe, a gift from his sister. He had visited Copenhagen for two weeks, and Paris for seven. In the daytime he swam in the pool—not the Seine, since it was already polluted—and at night he danced. A Nigerian friend took Father somewhere to get hash that was out of this world, but the boss wouldn't let him inside. The Nigerian got into a ritual knife fight and, when he brought the stuff out, hundreds of people followed Father wherever he walked.

Father hitchhiked to Madrid, Barcelona, and Tangiers. He got all kinds of dangerous drugs from the Mafia for free, and he knew that their plan was to get him hooked. Mother was shocked that Father could be so stupid. Father said no, everybody knew that you just take a little at a time, not too often, and you'll be OK.

By then Mother realized how far they had fallen from suitable conversations on the holy *Shabbat*—in the Holy Land, even—and started yelling that Father was stupid, and how could his sister have paid for that ridiculous trip! Father said Mother was just like his sister—meaning not cool—and left the table to take a nap, and Mother would have followed him with a barrage of insults if she hadn't needed to say psalms and finish her daily hour conversing with G-d.

Let's go back to Joseph. No one expected anything good to come from the son of these parents. One day, Joseph's friend Dan refused to get into his parents' car and visit his grandfather for *Shabbat*, so Joseph snatched the chance to invite him over. Joseph baked fresh bread, made a clean bed, prepared drinks, snacks, and games, and waited for Dan to arrive for the first *Shabbat* meal.

Dan didn't come.

Joseph looked everywhere in the settlement that night. When he finally found Dan in an abandoned trailer, Joseph tried to coax him out with potato chips and cola. Dan wouldn't come, and the longer Joseph stayed, the worse things got in the trailer. As the Sages say, association with bad company rubs off.

Thus, when the police arrived the next day, Dan and the other kids in the trailer pointed at Joseph.

I won't go into details of the radio broadcast, the investigating psychiatrist's report, the accusations of settlers and social workers, Joseph's expulsion from *yeshiva*, the family's eviction from the settlement, and the monolithic refusal of every respectable *yeshiva* in the Negev to accept even one student from this family. Only one school did accept Joseph—the only one that never confiscated the cell phones of parents and children, or their televisions and internet connections at home. One year after Joseph left, that *yeshiva* closed. Some say it was Divine Retribution. OK, I won't argue. Some say the parents should have left the Negev and moved to *Bnai Brak*.

A few years later, Joseph did resurface in the holy city of *Bnai Brak*, standing tall in his black hat and suit. He was the only student from the trailers chosen by the great *Rosh Yeshiva* of the generation, who happened to have a niece of marriageable age. She was not the most beautiful, but so what?

And so, this Joseph, whose brothers knew nothing of *yeshivas*, but all made their place with the paratroopers in Israel and the backpackers in Nepal, whose American English-speaking parents understood nothing about this Hebrew-speaking country; this Joseph miraculously arrived at a high, secure, and enviable position.

Or so it seemed.

Perhaps the marriage would not have run into trouble if Joseph's parents understood the Israeli mentality. I mean, the girl grew up in *Bnai Brak* and would have certainly told her parents that Joseph's brothers—at home for *Shabbat* in the Negev—read the secular newspapers and sat around in t-shirts and shorts.

Let's say she told. So, her parents got worried: *Don't go there. Bad company rubs off. Stay in* Bnai Brak.

And the girl moved back to her parents' house.

Joseph came to get her, and they sent him away.

The rabbi got involved, and another rabbi, and another, and all the talk just made things worse.

Not because Joseph had done something wrong, not because his parents had done anything wrong. It's just as the Sages say, that you acquire Israel by suffering.

My First Day in Monterey by Nina Kossman

On my first day in Monterey, I walk into a white-washed building on Pacific Street. Black letters above the entrance inform me that this is a hotel, and a clerk at a small desk says, You won't find anything cheaper that's also decent enough for a nice girl like yourself, so I pay him thirty dollars for a single room. He asks, Do you need any help with your luggage, and I show him my backpack and he says, This is not what I mean by luggage.

After I pay him, I have forty dollars left in my pocket and I feel rich. I walk down Pacific Street and stare at restaurant windows and at all the people sitting there behind glass and eating as if it were the most natural thing in the world for them. The possibility of eating in a restaurant doesn't occur to me, because, although I am rich and hungry, restaurants are for the super wealthy, those who have money to throw away to the wind.

When I walk into Safeway, the nearest supermarket, I am presented with more possibilities than I can stomach. After a long deliberation in the fruit aisle, I choose a small box of strawberries, and from a long row of some fifty varieties of cheese I get something called Havarti. I choose it because it is sliced, and I can eat it in my room without a knife. Cheese in my right hand, strawberries in my left, I stand in line at a cash register when I hear Russian speech behind me. I turn around and see a man unloading groceries from a cart back onto a Safeway shelf, saying to a small blond woman next to him, We don't need this. And we don't need that. And that. And that. I can't see his companion's face, but from her tense neck I can tell that she isn't happy with the way he is emptying the cart of all the things she was looking forward to tasting. What does the body need to support the mind, says the man, except milk, bread, eggs, and a nice chunk of meat? He puts the four necessities on the counter next to my supper.

I point at my meager provisions and say, This is my first day in Monterey.

The man looks at me and says, Let me guess. I bet you arrived from one of the centers of so-called civilization in order to work in the stable here with all our other Russian stable boys and girls.

No, I'm going to work at the Defense Language Institute as a Russian instructor.

That's what I'm talking about. The DLI is one big stable, and all the stable boys and girls hate each other's guts and are ready to eat each other alive, which is only natural of course.

I ask him if he's talking about students, and he says, No, God help us, certainly not. Students are one's friends, the only friends and supporters one has in this terrible, terrible place.

So I figure he's talking about teachers, and he says, Oh, yes, if you want to, you can call them teachers. I ask if they hate each other's guts because immigrants from the third wave hate immigrants from the second wave, and immigrants from the second wave hate immigrants from the third wave and the first wave—that is, if there are any first wavers still alive on this earth. I know this bit of history. First-wavers fled Russia during and right after the Bolshevik revolution; second-wavers fled during World War Two, and they are mostly ethnic Russians who were forced by Germans to work for the Third Reich, or had been captured by the Germans and survived and became DPs, displaced persons, after the war; and the third-wavers—well, I'm one of them—and this man and his blond woman friend are also third-wavers, those of us who left in the seventies. Jews, or Russians who married Jews to emigrate and to free the one-sixth of the world's surface of our unwanted Semitic presence.

He says, It's not because of the waves, or because of this or that, it's because of the rotten human nature that everybody is ready to eat each other alive. He waits for the blond woman to pay for their purchases and as soon as she's done, he says, Goodbye and take care of yourself, and the woman turns her thin pink face to me for the first time and says, Goodbye. They leave the store, and I walk back to my cheap little room in the whitewashed hotel on Pacific Street.

In my room I spend some time contemplating a crumpled note I have fished from my pocket. In the note my mother reminds me to call the Levitins, my parents' acquaintances from our long-ago time in Rome. Rome was the in-between place for Soviet refugees waiting for American visas, and that was where my parents and the Levitins met, and talked, and visited some of the ruins and churches that all tourists had to visit, although my parents and the Levitins were not tourists and not even citizens of any of the countries that supply the world with its hordes of tourists. Now the Levitins work at the DLI. My parents called them from New York to tell them I was coming, and could I stay with them until I found my own place, and the Levitins said why not, have her call us once she is here in Monterey. Well, now I'm here in Monterey and I have the note with the Levitins' phone number in my mother's precise handwriting, and I consume my feast of cheese and strawberries, thinking about the unknown future that awaits me in this brightly-colored town.

PART TWO

The change is slow

Throwing Down Roots by Amit Majmudar

WHEN I WAS six years old, I swallowed an apple seed. My mom screamed for my dad, and together they marched me by my elbows, like a dissident in the old country, into the backyard. Did I feel it? Was it coming? I nodded, and they made me drop my pants and squat. I strained until a knobby tree root emerged with a drop of blood. The root kept emerging, digging into the hard Ohio soil where our ancestors had never sunk a spade and I stomped it in deeper with a boot. Now tilt your head up, sobbed my dad, and say the prayers. What prayers? I asked. The prayers I taught you, damn it. But he was a chemical engineer and had never taught me any prayers. So, my mom had me gargle water instead. The gods can't tell the difference, she assured me. That modest watering was all it took for the top half of the tree to shoot out of my throat and open its leafy umbrella. Sing something, sobbed my mom, so I sang the national anthem around the trunk that shot through me. The branches grew apples, and the apples reddened. The trunk swelled, too, cracking my ribcage. I had lost sensation in my legs by then, and in my chest, and in my arms. I kept singing around the tree trunk even though I myself couldn't make out the words. The sound called all the kids in the neighborhood to our backyard, and my parents fled indoors and called the police. When the police didn't answer, they called the old country. I was still squatting, still with my pants around my ankles. The laughing kids used my knees as steps to climb my apple tree and snatch the apples. They didn't take any home to their moms to bake into pies. They just ate the apples right there and made me watch as they savored the juice, as my red delicious blood trickled over their chins and down their wrists. I must have tasted like the real thing.

Arrivals by Irina Popescu

WE GOT HERE and ate a lot of *Iron Kids* bread. Disgusting and delicious and cheap, like our new life in America where no one understands my name. I tell Mama I want to change it every day, but she insists I'm being a baby. I'm tired of being an immigrant and often wonder about the connection between infancy and immigration. Is there one beyond the *i*? I think it's time to go home but I don't know how to move between these points, so I follow snail paths on concrete and hope.

A baby changes your life deliberately. A baby changes your life by not. Not sleeping. Not eating. Not doing. Not speaking. Not knowing. Not being you though she was once you, he was once you, they was once you. Now, no longer. Not. The change is slow. The change is a negation of being. The change involves precision and cutting and butchering until the new life has space outside of you. You, the mother who promises to be nothing like her mother. The not mother. You, the mother who turns away from her mother, thinking you can do things better, thinking you must, thinking that now is your turn to shine and construct and rebuild. Now in this not. But sand-castles can't be built without water and you are always thirsty.

I need to tell you the secret I've been keeping: I meant only half of the things, the half that looked lemony and salty like a bruised seashore somewhere off the Santa Monica pier where I dreamt my first kiss and realized tongues taste like snails, only sweeter.

I was not old enough to understand changes. Yet, I knew enough about the world to transition from you to me and back again, our stupid orbits out of orbit, so that when you pretended not to hear I knew you heard because you could always hear the words of the songs I listened to on my headphones even when the volume was low. Your arrival into my life sparkled. Then the burning happened, but only after, only after, only after.

She thinks she knows everything but she's just a kid, she tells my father over dinner. *She wants to change her name. Have you heard of something so crazy? Her name? Sometimes she's too much.*

When I push in the *Iron Kids* bread it stays down and makes no sound.

I know a lot about the world. I know that people are too lazy to open doors, so everything opens automatically, and reflection stops. I know that now I eat Dave's Killer multigrain bread and it costs $5.50 and if you buy two loaves that means you are spending over ten dollars on bread and that says something about the kind of person you are. My son loves smashed avocado toast with sea salt and sesame seeds and he is only two. I think he is becoming a person. My son has a name to mark his difference. I gave him that name knowing that he would spend moments in his life writing out potential names. Easy names. Names people can spell and pronounce, names that erase me.

Green beans fall to the floor and I think of my Mama's nickname for me when I was nine and scared. *Settle down, green bean.* I did start settling down each time she spoke because it felt wrong to make her the witness to my spiraled mind. *We aren't illegal humans, we just don't have everything we need to belong here permanently.* Is there a connection between green beans and permanence? I thought that when we had the magic papers, making us the version of human we lost across the Atlantic, a portal would open in time. Time. *Give it time*, she told and retold me, until I decided to go looking for time. Where is she? I tell her I'm ready to give her what she needs but time ignores me and all she leaves me with is difference.

Lacey? Is the name I gave myself in coffee shops across Central Texas to minimize my difference, and often when they called it, I would forget the sounds because how can you remember the name that is not yours when it is called aloud? I imagine my Mama trying to pronounce my new name, *Le-a-cci*, in a foreign tone, sparking illegibility.

He didn't cry when he was born. He didn't cry and they had to make him cry, and then he did cry. It was the first sound he made and the most terrible.

Your name is you. We named you this because you were the only peace in our lives during the worst part of the war. You didn't cry when you were born, and your Aunt said yours is a good omen for a light beginning. That's where your name comes from. This is my new beginning in the West. My new beginning as his mother who is not her mother but who learns motherhood as a craft handed down.

I make green beans and sausage for dinner and he eats them by slurping out the beans and leaving the carcass. The sausage he devours smiling, throwing pieces on the floor, *pentru morti*, Mama would say, *for the dead.* She, mashing potatoes for our special-treat-Sunday-night dinner, while opening salty meat called SPAM that cost sixty-six cents at Kroger. It tastes okay for jellied rectangle meat. I can't tell what parts of what animals it's born from. I think about peace.

I have lived South-West-East, three points on an invented map with all different-same places enclosing people who smile and others who won't. I see her putting plates filled with cloudy mashed potatoes on the table. She deliberately cuts SPAM on the nice serving tray we got from the thrift store for eighty cents and puts it in the middle of the table. I become her.

Chasing Gods by Edvin Subašić

We reach the camp at dusk, exhausted from a long journey. The light bulbs glow yellow and warm. In the past two years, I've seen electrical light on only a few occasions. The power is off. The war is on. We're in the middle of it, watching, listening, from the outside in.

Our sanctuary appears from behind a row of linden trees on the outskirts of a small town in Croatia—a crumbling two-storied warehouse. In front of it I see the crisscrossed clotheslines strung between the patio columns and the trees across the yard, weighed down by damp attire of all sorts. White linen sheets and cloth diapers welcome us as we enter the courtyard. Kids scream and run around the swaying clothes, teasing and chasing. The babies coo and cry in their parents' arms. Men and women hang in little clusters like parched currants, dangling dry in the autumn twilight. Some casually leaning against a wall or post, listening and shrugging. Some talking and gesticulating, spitting on the ground furiously.

Humanity is drowning in desperation and desire, in its own smell of stale fear, soiled diapers, and laundry detergent. Women, men, children, elders, politicians, thieves, policemen, and sex offenders—brought together and crowded inside the temporary shelter. Smokers, drinkers, lovers, and storytellers. They are all there—sitting, squatting, standing.

Some whispering—anxiously conferring—and some playing chess or cards. They stride about the building, roaming aimlessly up and down, leaving, returning, waiting in line for supper—mostly silent, only their children lively and fearless.

The day our German sponsors greet us, we are welcomed in their home with warm friendly smiles, fresh homemade *Apfelkuchen* and hot coffee on the table. I stand still mid-step and picture the moment again, eight years later, in a story I'm writing. The unbearable love toward fellow humans—its awkwardness, its undeniable existence—and the years of war propel me into future.

I drive into Portland in my ancient Nissan, its trunk filled with clothes and books. The greatest literary magazine of all time lies in the passenger seat—ten copies piled on top of each other. The gods smiled upon me just when I started believing that I'd used up all my luck back home running from the spear of Ares. Finally, after years of submitting and receiving only form rejections my story is on page 43 of *The Cottage*. It's my story, a story of an immigrant who has nothing to do—no immigrant life such as working several jobs, serving generations of Americans, proving himself to his own little god that now lives among all the American gods. Oh, God bless *The Cottage*.

It's 3 o'clock. I'm early. I'm supposed to meet my friend, Miro, after five, when he gets off work. I drive to Powell's Books, park in a back alley across from the freeway, and walk into the bookstore. Powell's is a world of its own. I enter the Blue Room: literature, poetry, small press, classics. I skim through the tall rows brimming with books. This world is cozy; I could get old here. I browse through literary magazines. At last, I'm in one of them. I remember the advice every editor gives. They say to read the magazine to know if my writing fits. In my case, I should just give up. But I'm here, and I want to be read. For a silly yet selfish reason every writer secretly harbors, I want to be heard. I want to prove it to my little god—the one I betrayed and left dying years ago. As I contemplate this, two young couples on the other side of the aisle burst into laughter. I step closer. They're young, they're beautiful, and they're white; they're white in a way I will never be.

One of the young women is holding Kerouac, the other Austen. The men are still undecided. Something keeps me from stepping away. I'm watching a movie; they're Hollywood—gorgeous and clever. I pretend I'm reading as I listen to their jokes, Henry Miller in my hand by accident. I don't get them, as if they speak Hungarian. I wonder. I wonder about their American lives. Their language is impeccable. They're so clean. They smell like a citrus grove, overpowering the book scent.

Fifteen minutes later, they step out of the bookstore. I pay $6.75 for a used copy of *The Colossus of Maroussi* and follow. I'm right behind them. They don't feel me. They cross the street and continue talking. They don't use their hands; their bodies are erect and smooth. I close in on them. I've never done this in my life. I'm not one of those Peeping Thomases. But I want, so want, to know where they're going. They still discuss literature and writing. They talk Faulkner and Woolf, form, craft, style—the essence and existence. Everything is there. They mention Ginsberg, they reference Plath. I still hope. I want to hear them say it or at least a hint that they know it: *There's a world out there. It's dirty, it's foreign, and people live there, too. Their children know how to play. Their children are gods.*

Six blocks later, they enter a Thai restaurant. They sit by the window. I stand ten yards away by the crosswalk, leaning against a light post, pretending I'm waiting for the green light to cross. The white man lights up, his legs spread, soon turning into digits. They look out the window and freeze for a moment, glancing at me in unison before they return to their discussion. Their wine and appetizers arrive. They gleam over the abundance in front of them. The sun sinks behind the new, silver building across the street. I brush my fingers along the cold metal post and let my hand slip. I turn away and step ahead, clutching Miller in my armpit. The traffic light is red again.

Illegals are the Best Drivers by Erick Messias

ILLEGALS ARE THE best drivers, when a traffic stop means a ticket back to Guatemala instead of a warning.

Martinez said, "You drive well, *cabrón*!"

Between Gabriel's Portuguese and Martinez's Spanish, the best common language was still English.

Gabriel took the keys to Martinez's delivery van. He had carried such keys carelessly back in Brazil, yet these felt so different. They meant more money, along with the risk of the two men's common nightmare of deportation.

God knows how he and Mayra needed the extra cash now.

Most days and nights, Gabriel was the driver for Martinez's Tacos & Fajitas de Oro. Each catering event was a risk, but his driving record remained spotless. Not a single change of lane without a blinker, not a mile above the speed limit. Navigating the maze between Queens and the Bronx during rush hour was a breeze compared to driving at the Yellow Line in Rio de Janeiro any time of the day. At least here, you did not have to try to guess who to trust at each stop. Who would it be, the police or the gangs?

Now, Mayra was pregnant. They had come all the way from Brazil through different lanes and had ended up knocking Margaritas back at a party in Spanish Harlem, the only two Hispanics there unable to speak Spanish. They gravitated to each other that night, and every opportunity since then.

"You are my little piece of Brazil in New York," Mayra had told him, looking deep into his green eyes.

As she became bigger with their child, they looked for prenatal care. Community health centers, medical school clinics, any place that did not ask too many questions and appeared clean. Mayra settled on the Harmony Clinic where luck, or perhaps *Nossa Senhora Aparecida*, the patron saint of Brazil, had placed a Brazilian intern who had been an obstetrician for a few years in the Amazon.

The big day came in the middle of night. They had slept for the past week in the restaurant, where they could access the van at any time. Gabriel took the wheel, and Mayra lay down in the back seat, where she did the breathing exercises. And the baby began to fight his way out into the world.

For the first time, Gabriel went over the speed limit. Soon, blue lights were trailing behind them, down the avenue. His mind was too chaotic to consider his options; as if by instinct, he flipped the right blinker and pulled out of the lane.

The flashlight hit his green eyes like the Brazilian sun of his childhood.

"Sir, I have no papers. *Sin documentos*." Blinded by the light, he waited for what was to come.

"What's going on?"

"It's my wife. She's about to deliver our son."

The flashlight turned a long ellipse to the backseat. Mayra took deep breaths, moaning quietly.

"You follow me."

The policeman walked back to the cruiser, keeping his blue lights rotating like *porta-bandeiras* in the *Carnaval* parade. He drove past the van; Gabriel pulled out, and they moved together, a two-car motorcade in the mostly empty streets.

In a few minutes, Gabriel saw the neon signs of the emergency room. He drove through the car entrance, where paramedics were waiting for them. As he closed the van door, he saw the police cruiser disappear in the night, the officer's arm outside signaling a thumbs-up.

To celebrate Joaquim's baptism, the crew came together at the same roof in Spanish Harlem where Gabriel and Mayra had first met.

"It was not *Nossa Senhora Aparecida*! She does not come this far. It was *Lupe, amigo*!" Martinez lifted his beer to the patron saint of Mexico, the Virgin of Guadalupe.

Gabriel smiled at his compadre and raised his glass.

"Here is to the heroes of that most blessed night. My ladies: Mayra; the officer—a man, yes, but Lady Liberty in uniform—and our ladies of Aparecida and Guadalupe, who all worked together."

Martinez grinned. "And to your man—your Joaquim, the one who needs no visa or green card."

Lido by James Corpora

ONE OF HIS arms was shorter than the other but no one noticed this, and I don't think he was aware of it himself. The right was the stronger—I remember the right—but the left, too, and I remember how he swung them in front of him as he walked. Swung them easily as if his hands were rubber balls on the end of strips and his forearms fulcrums. He wore a hat in those days, the kind worn by immigrant laborers working in the fields and on the roads and highways of the country, building it. He was a laborer, and he was an immigrant, but one who had grown up here. The hat was battered with a blue sweatband. He wore it all the time.

He worked with a shovel and a pick and the hat was for the sun. Later he was an entrepreneur and small businessman. He had a little red truck he drove all over town and I remember the way he shifted gears, very gently so as not to break the truck's insides. His relations with people were easy as well—so as not to break their insides—but sometimes he did anyway, not meaning to. He broke insides. He did not break my insides, but he bent them a little and sometimes I wish he hadn't.

I remember the truck, the pick, and a gold trumpet he bought me when I was twelve years old. There was also a fancy bike with fenders and a horn. The bike cost him sixty-five dollars, and the trumpet was about the same. He was able to afford neither at the time, so it was nice of him to buy these things for me. I appreciated them. But the way he bent me with them later, and the way he kept reminding me of the sixty-five-dollar gold trumpet he couldn't afford, and the bike with fenders I didn't really want because bikes with fenders were out of style then, hurt me.

The gold trumpet was especially hurtful, the way he used it and the way it bent me, my insides. I took it and learned to play it but never really had a talent for the instrument. I didn't have the lip. I practiced for hours anyway, but I was no Miles Davis and not able to really play the thing, only practice it.

He heard about a scholarship one day. A friend told him, and then he told me. He said we would go together to this military school on the far side of town and I would audition for it. "I can't play anything," I told him. "I have nothing memorized. I can't play anything even if it is right in front of me."

"That's okay," he replied. "We'll audition anyway. You might get a scholarship."

A scholarship to this school, a military academy, where the kids wore uniforms and were probably rich. I didn't want to audition because I couldn't play anything but scales. I also thought he might be trying to get rid of me somehow. It was cheaper to have me out of the house and someone else feeding me. Even though I did not eat much then, or drink anything but milk, food was expensive in those days.

We climbed into the truck and drove across town at night; I remember it was at night and in the wintertime. The far side of L.A. at night. The streets were slick and I had the trumpet in its case on the seat beside me. When we reached the school, we drove in through the big double gates in front and up to an ivy-covered building where we parked the truck. We went inside and found the man auditioning kids for open positions in the school band. "Full tuition and full scholarship," he said to me.

"Sir," I replied, "I can't play anything."

He smiled.

"Nothing?"

"No, sir. Nothing. Scales is all."

He was a big, heavyset guy in shirtsleeves and gold-rimmed glasses. I remember the glasses and the light in them, and I remember his smile. He must have heard a hundred kids that day, all of them with flashy instruments and capable of playing any number of tunes from memory, "Canadian Capers," for example, or "Flight of the Bumble Bee."

"Well, play a scale for me then," he said.

I took out my music, played a scale, and he thanked us very politely, the way a man in a position of some power would thank an immigrant and his kid for coming all that way to play a scale when other kids were playing "Flight of the Bumble Bee" from memory and doing a lot of double-tonguing on their instruments the way the kids in LA double-tongued in those days. I could barely play a scale, let alone double-tongue, and I did not have the lip.

We packed up the trumpet, got into the truck, and drove all the way across town again. I was bent a little on the inside but not broken, put slightly off-course in my life perhaps because of that session with the heavyset man in shirtsleeves, but not entirely sunk or scuttled yet, even though my insides would never be the same.

A couple of years later, when I was ready to quit the instrument, Lido said to me, "Well, maybe you should quit it, maybe it's time. But it's been a valuable experience for you and one I'm sure you'll never forget."

He was right. It was, and I haven't.

I'll be Back by Varya Kartishai

Most of my dreams are unremarkable, but sometimes I have the good fortune to find myself standing on that street again. On the best nights of all I have a pick in my hands, and I lose no time, swinging it high into the air to drive its point into the dull asphalt. After a few blows, blue-gray cobbles and the shining steel of trolley tracks begin to appear. The street as it was pours out from between the stones like smoke and builds itself around me.

I work feverishly, my hands bleeding from the rough wood handle, as the past returns like some twentieth century Brigadoon. The steps appear first, glowing deep rose in the sunlight, then the brick houses, and a door opens in one. A small child appears, followed by an old woman's voice, "*Gay arois*, go out, *shpiel*, play. *Gay nit in dem street*." She looks around her—there are no other children, but a woman is approaching with a patched string bag full of vegetables. The child watches as a slender carrot works its way past a patch and onto the sidewalk. At last, the carrot has fallen, and it can begin:

Run down, child, pick up the carrot, run after the woman with the beautifully embroidered scarf covering her dark hair. Say, "Stop, please, this is yours." She looks blank and keeps on going. Tug her long black skirt and wave the carrot at her. She says, "*Teşekkur ederim*," smiles, and takes the carrot. That is not what Bubbie says; does it mean thank you? Follow her to her house, only a few doors away, and watch her go in. As the door closes behind her, a spicy aroma lingers in the air. Run up the steps, knock on the door, and when she opens it, ask, "What are you cooking?" She doesn't understand, so make sniffing noises, say "Mmm" and lick your lips, shameless child. Now she says, "*Et suyu*," then says, "*buyurun*," and motions you inside, smiling.

Follow her to the kitchen. She pulls out a chair and ladles some soup into a bowl for you. Try to say what she said for the carrot; it isn't the same, but she is pleased, this lonely woman in a strange country. The soup, *et suyu*, is unfamiliar but delicious. There are pots of herbs on the windowsill, like Bubbie's herbs, but the leaves and smells are not the same. Stay for a little while, as she points to things and gives you her words for them, and you return your words for them to her. Then go back to your own house to eat black bread and cheese.

Afterward, start to go out, but Bubbie stops you; "*Dof gayn* in Doctor, you *mus shtayen mit Pani. Kum*." She takes your hand—you go down the street, and cross with her to the other side, where you can't go by yourself. The door is opened by a small, round, old woman with a white kerchief on her hair. Bubbie hikes up her skirt and pulls out a purse from her petticoat pocket. She hands some silver to the old woman, tells you, "*Shtay. Ich* come back," and leaves you. You follow Pani down the hall to the kitchen. She has herbs on the sill too, but different ones. A shelf covered with a lacy scarf hangs on the wall. It holds a red candle burning in front of a picture of a pretty lady with a blue scarf and a gold circle behind her head. At the table a small blond boy is eating something that smells wonderful. You point, and Pani says, "Want *prockes*?" She gives you a plate of cabbage rolled around rice in a red sauce—so good. The boy is Leon—when he finishes eating, he says, "Come see the rabbits." They are outside in a wire cage, but their ears droop and they look sad. After a while, Bubbie comes to take you home.

But what is that noise? The big truck with the fires of hell burning under the cauldron is coming down the street. It is laying asphalt over the cobbles. I shriek, "No! We have not visited the *Signora* who makes *strufoli* and dresses her beautiful *fico* tree for winter in her husband's old coat. We have to see Degiz, our Armenian lady who grows peaches that perfume the whole room and drip juice down your chin." I cry out and throw my arms wide apart to stop the truck, but it comes on, pressing me down into the hole I have so painfully dug. The asphalt covers my face, and I can no longer breathe the air of the past. I wake in the drab now with tears streaming from my eyes.

But I will go back. I will. Wait for me, Bubbie, Pani, Hanim, Signora, Degiz.

Wait for me.

Living Out Loud by Yong Takahashi

He left me because I slammed the kitchen cabinet door. The term "irretrievably broken" on the divorce filing was insufficient for him. He wrote "other" on top of the front page, then proceeded to explain I was too loud to live with.

My husband filled out the paperwork and filed it with the court. In his mind, he had done his part.

"The least you can do is to show up for the hearing. Only one of us is required to make an appearance," he said.

Open hours for divorce court are on Tuesdays from noon to two p.m. I enter the courtroom where only a clerk is present. She informs me the judge is at lunch in his chambers, and he will sign off on my paperwork there.

"Hello," I whisper as I knock tentatively on the judge's door.

"Come on in," says a gruff voice.

"Can you sign my divorce papers?" I stand in the doorway until he waves me in.

"Where's your counsel?" he asks while eating his club sandwich.

"I don't have an attorney." I bite my lip.

Rolling his eyes, he grabs the petition out of my hand. He asks me if there is any chance of reconciliation, although my husband has written across the front page NO CHANCE

OF GETTING BACK TOGETHER with his favorite Sharpie marker.

I can tell he was angry by the way he wrote his letters—each word progressively getting thicker as his anger bubbled to the surface.

DON'T SLAM THE FRONT DOOR was printed on bright yellow stock paper and glued to the daylight window in our foyer.

STOP SLAMMING THE CABINET DOORS was written on several index cards and taped all over the kitchen.

YOU'RE TOO LOUD was smeared with red lipstick on my bathroom mirror.

The judge's question is only a formality. His pity washes over me and I can't look at him. I shake my head.

"Why didn't you ask for anything?"

"He said it would be easier this way."

"Mrs. Mallory, I shouldn't give you legal advice, but do you want to counter with a cruelty charge?"

I blush. My husband conditioned me to pause—to be afraid—to watch my volume and to think everything through before speaking. I touch my throat to soften my tone.

"No, your honor, I just want it to be over. Ten years of silence is more than enough."

"Alright then. I grant your divorce." The judge signs the decree and hands it back to me. "Take it to the clerk for filing. Good luck."

"Thank you," I whisper.

I hand the documents to the clerk. The ladies behind the counter see what my husband has written, and they snicker.

"You should get a certified copy in a few weeks, Mrs. Mallory." The woman slides the receipt through the window.

"It's Michelle." I look down and smile.

I run to the parking garage, my heels pounding on the pavement. I haven't heard that sound in such a long time.

I accidentally hit the alarm on my car remote. I panic and I look around for him. After a few seconds, I know he's not there. I slam the door closed. I take a deep breath, without worrying that my sinuses are too loud.

I enter my new apartment and let the door close, naturally. "Boom!" I chuckle.

I throw my keys onto the glass tabletop and the chime echoes throughout the living room. I throw up my arms. "Score!"

I pull a plate out of the kitchen cabinet. The dishes are not separated by parchment paper to dull the clinking. The cabinet doors do not have a slow release hinge like my ex-husband installed at the house. I let the handle fall from my fingers. The door ricochets a few times off the frame. I do a dance of joy.

I grab a knife from the silverware tray and scoop peanut butter out of the jar. The knife scrapes the sides. Scrape. Scrape. Scrape.

I throw the knife into the sink, which I did not line with a rubber mat. The knife torpedoes and scratches the stainless steel. I twirl around like I did when I was a little girl.

I chomp the sandwich, slurp my Coke, and slam the plate on the counter with glee.

My arms sway over my head. And the crowd cheers.

Learning to Float by Jose Varghese

"First, you learn to float, Samir."

He's too young to learn, or to understand my words. But he loves it when I hold him horizontal so that the waves lap against his back and tease his limbs. He giggles and moves spasmodically in all directions.

There is an ocean to cross, my son, between that feeling of being cradled by the water beneath your body and the backstrokes you achieve in due course, owning the water and splashing it all around you. It calls for an undying resilience to push everything behind.

"Stay still, Baba. Let me click once more,"Yara says.

She's standing behind me, admiring her new world, facing what's supposed to be her little brother's first swimming lesson with me. She has run away from her mom, abandoning a half-finished flatbread, to see us through her new lens.

I wish I could tell her that it's no use immortalizing such moments. She's proud of her craft, of carefully bringing together the strange and the beautiful within her frames and excluding any sight she considers ugly from what it encloses. She has been so ever since we were forced to escape a land, and a sea, that we used to call ours.

"The sea isn't the same everywhere, Baba. Look at these colours... It's bottle green. How I miss the turquoise of our shallow shores!"

"I guess it's the sun playing games, Yara, or it could be the water density. Why don't you look it up?" I suggest.

"Yes, I'll do it."

She's sure to find it out by herself and share it when we are all together. She's an expert at fact-hunting as a way of pushing away the unpleasant from the past to revel in the flamboyance of her present. She expects us to be like her.

"At least we're all together here, Baba, unlike many of my friends who got separated from their families," she said last week.

I never have the heart to tell her that I had to deal with more complex separations than that. I'll need a long time to shake off the memories of the sea that was mine. Or I may fail in that. She's too young to see my whole childhood, youth, relatives, friends, songs, books, food, epiphanies, that I had to drown to stay alive. She has better clues to her mother's losses.

But we must learn from Yara. She's the one who will find our way in the days to come in this strange land that has taken us, though with certain conditions, of course. "Melt like sugar in milk," making it sound easier and sweeter than it would ever be. But our losses shouldn't dampen Yara's spirits, as she's old enough, unlike Samir, to feel their weight from our eyes and sighs.

I can only float here, my girl, for you and your little brother.

"Perfect. See how the sun shines on you guys!" She shows us the photos that she took.

They look great. She has managed some candid shots as well, which seem to have captured our careless moments in unison with the waves. Samir's eyes widen as each new photo lights up the grey screen.

The Perfect Girl by Ruth Knafo Setton

THE PERFECT GIRL was born in America.

The perfect girl likes Dmitri Bolotovsky, who plays Rimsky-Korsakov like nobody's business, even though his butt jiggles when he runs, and his fingers are flat as piano keys. She does not waste time daydreaming about living in the House on the Hill with blond parents who speak English without an accent and don't embarrass her and pack lunches with sandwiches of Velveeta cheese in slices of spongy white bread instead of weird-smelling things wrapped in foil paper that fall apart the minute you pick them up. The perfect girl doesn't daydream at all, especially not when she's working in the family restaurant or doing her homework. She does not boss her little brother around or act impatient with her mother and aunt, does not smoke and does not insist that smoking her best friend Iris's Kools doesn't count because they're borrowed, does not dream of Tony River's blue-eyed smile that time she bumped into him in the hall because she knows it's hopeless and he's one of the wild boys who spends every afternoon in detention, does not ask the Ouija Board if Tony will break up with Steffi Rodriguez and love her instead; she definitely does not sneak into Iris's church and beg Jesus to make Tony like her, does not call herself Brittney when she has a perfectly good name of her own, does not bring home filthy, unclean food stuffed in cans, does not slump as if she's ashamed of her height, does not skip downstairs three at a time and land with a thud in the dining room, startling customers; she does not fight baths because she knows that boys like girls who are clean, does not fight shampoos because she knows that broccoli and carrots will sprout in her dirty scalp, does not spy on grown-ups, does not follow strangers because she finds them suspicious, or ask customers prying questions. She always locks the front door in case the enemy returns, never locks the door in case a lonely stranger wanders in, always asks a boy questions about himself while staring at a point in the center of his forehead and never looks away unless there is a tempest or typhoon and even then excuses herself graciously before lowering her eyes, always says no when she means yes, always leaves him wanting more, does not eat too much in front of him, even though she's always starving, does not wear glasses in front of him even though she always wants to see everything, does say please and thank-you, and does not make her grandfather roll over in his grave three times when he hears (from nosy Mrs. Warner) that she was seen kissing a strange man at the Winterville Fall Faire, even after explaining Iris was a witness that he offered her a twenty-dollar bill to kiss her and she simply had no choice but to do it for the experience.

No.

The perfect girl always knows the difference between right and wrong and is an example to her younger brother and a shining example of a perfect American girl, and she does not—she does—she always—she never—she is—she is not—the only thing we know for sure is that she is not me.

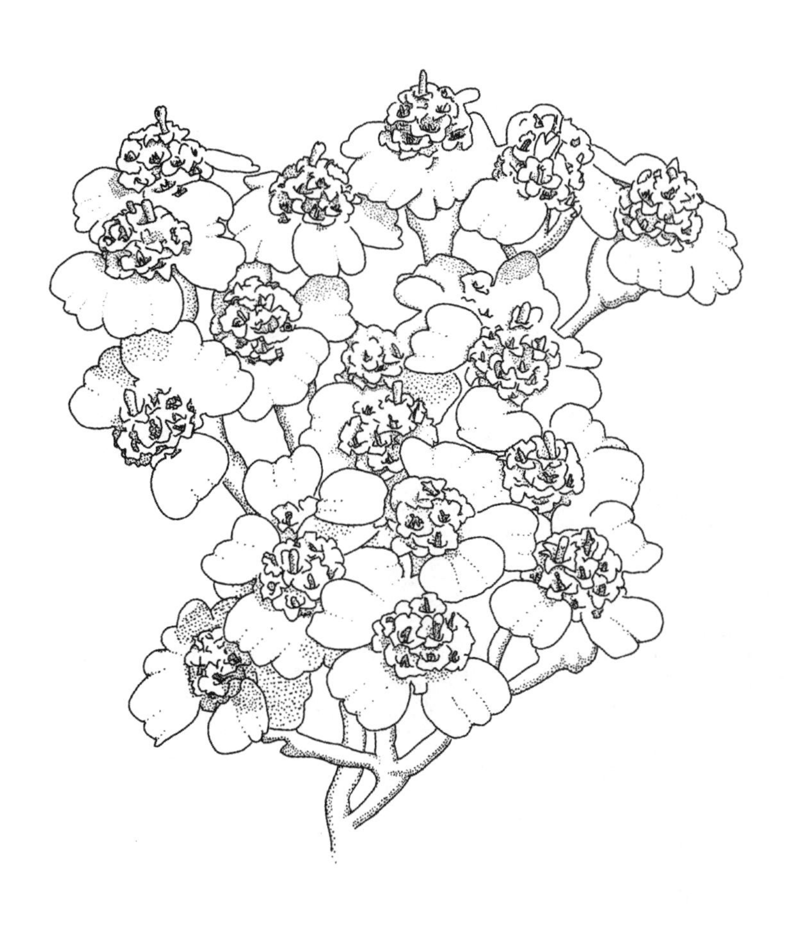

PART THREE

Inheriting the earth

Ventricular by Feliz Moreno

WHITE NOISE. SHE had shut off the radio, gotten tired of the *corridos* as she drove south on the I-5 toward the place she used to refer to as home. The sun had set, so she did not have to look at the rows and rows of produce stretched for miles over the Central Valley. Flat land. Sprawled out on either side of the interstate, from the San Joaquin to Kings County. Like the thread of a heart monitor machine, stretched until its peaks and valleys ceased to exist. *Nueces, uvas, maíz, almendras, fresas, chabacones*—Papá used to quiz her so that she knew all the crops grown in the 450-mile-long heart of the state. Now there was only darkness and the semitruck humming along on the road ahead of her.

Heart murmur. She was thinking about the extra electrical current of her heart. She imagined it as a misplaced spark in her pulmonary artery, the flicker of a lightbulb in a shoddily wired home. Arrhythmia, the doctor had called it, the word itself sounding like an affectionate murmur, a term of endearment: arrhyth-*mija*; arrhyth-*mi querida. Corazón malo*, her mother had called Papá's ailment, *sin remedio*. No remedy for the sour love between them, either. Her chest ached with the memory of her parents and the bad heart she had inherited from her father. Now she was on her way to retrieve him and his bad heart. All a pile of ash, in the end. To be collected, to be scattered, to be returned to the land he had spent so much time tending. She hadn't seen another car for miles when the trailer of the semitruck began to swivel, and her focus snapped.

A thumping in her chest. The semi drifted, the driver overcorrected, swerved left, then right. A screeching of rubber. She pounded the brake. An intake of breath. Groan of axle metal. A ripping of rubber. Screeching of brakes. Tires tipping. On its side, the truck crumpled like a chip bag. A whoosh of water and fruit. *Tomates*. Transported in water to prevent bruising. To keep the skin from turning dark purplish-blue. The static flash of metal meeting asphalt breaking the darkness. The scraping of the trailer as it dragged. The tinkling of a million pieces of glass scattering over the road.

Her ears rang. Engines hissed. She smelled gasoline. How had she made it past the truck unscathed? The last few seconds like a buried memory. She pulled over to the shoulder. In her rearview mirror she could not see the truck driver anywhere. Someone was screaming. Tomatoes rolled. They slurped beneath her feet as she exited the car, juice running off the road, into her eyes. She could barely see them in the dark, these rubies of the valley scattered over the interstate. Legs shaking, she fell to her knees. Her chest ached.

She picked up the tomato next to her, the skin textured and dripping where it had split open. She balanced it in her hand, studied it, dizzy with adrenaline. The fruit was dense, purplish-blue in the moonlight. It was so strange. She stared at it, held it at a distance from her collapsed body. It had valves, arteries, veins. Her eyes adjusted to the dark and she could make out the outline of a vena cava, an aorta. It pulsed in her palm, juice flowing over her arm. The emptiness in her chest became visceral as she realized that it even had an extra electrical pulse, a murmur that echoed in her ears.

The Ravine by Genia Blum

KIEV

In September, the foliage turned yellow and red. Bodies fell, clothed only in fear, into the ravine, the pit, the abyss.

Naked flesh on naked flesh, warm blood, excrement—hell stinking beneath sand and earth.

All night, the bonfires flared, smoke rising into God's desolate kingdom; a hundred thousand souls and more, tracing runes between the stars.

MUNICH

Every evening after vespers, as altar candles flickered, pious sisters hunched over stacks of newspapers in the cloister's vaulted hall, scissors opening and closing, snip-snip, click-clack.

They'd warned the children not to play in the *verboten* ruin that separated *Schloss* Nymphenburg from their reinstated convent school. Lucifer could snatch them up and drag them to an inferno under the crater where an Allied bomb had hit the palace. The attack destroyed the royal chapel, converted by the Nazis to an infirmary, and *Mater* Sekundilla had perished, as did a nameless patient who'd survived the Eastern Front.

The school's lavatory was an unlit purgatory: wet floors, no soap or towels, no toilet roll, only unfinished wooden boxes filled with squares of inky newsprint—reminders of the trivial deprivations of the recent war.

Wimpled nuns worked their rusty shears, and Jesus glared from His crucifix on the wall, begrudging His forgiveness, tallying each snip-snip, click-clack.

WINNIPEG

The name escaped their throats with a soft, fricative "G." They'd christened their daughter "Evgenia" in a ceremony at Saints Vladimir and Olga Cathedral, but always addressed her by the diminutive "Genia," with the inflection that led people to assume they were mispronouncing the far more common "Jeannie." In school, the teacher called her that in class, which made her feel pleasantly ordinary, and the same schoolteacher suggested her parents stop speaking Ukrainian at home, warning them of the foreign accent their daughter would acquire.

Never. Her mother bristled. *We lost everything else.*

After the war, they'd rescued consonants, vowels, a trail of syllables. They spoke and prayed in their mother tongue, worshipped God in a church erected by immigrants, and denied the concept of collective blame.

The hymns and litany of the Divine Liturgy resound in a gilded nave; the sun pierces stained-glass windows exalting rulers and saints, The Blessed Virgin of the Cossacks, Kiev's Golden Domes.

Illuminated by colored light, dust ascends into incense-filled air: ashes from across the ocean, from the ravine, the scar, the abyss, where flakes of white bone remain.

Dust Day by Aida Bode

The empty house made me feel like the small fly of summer, lost and confused, buzzing to find shade and shelter. I had anticipated this moment, but never its loneliness, its absolute silence and abandonment. The noise was gone now—all the commotion, the disbelief, the pain, the tears. Even the weather was sunny, the way she would have wanted it. The window was open, and the wind was blowing the white lace curtains. I noticed my reflection on the glass of the dresser in the dark corner of her room, making me think that you need darkness to see yourself. There I was, a faint reflection of pale skin, hazel eyes, dimly pinked lips, and black curly hair.

The room behind me seemed like a one-dimensional blue, where walls lost their corners. The bed, done the way she kept it, the white cover she had crocheted for her dowry decorated with the pillows I embroidered, their colors lost in the dark glass. The weakly red chandelier that my grandfather had designed, looking as if it was attached to an invisible ceiling. Farther away the mahogany nightstands seemed blurred in the dim air, and the open door—in front of which I'd been standing for the past few minutes—looked like an entryway to another reality.

As the curtain danced on the wind, it created shapes of light that cruised my body. I crossed my hands over my shoulders and stared as the light stood on my fingers. I couldn't hold it, but it could hold me.

I walked out of the room hoping that light would follow me, and it did. It caressed my back, my legs, my feet, and walked with me to the corridor. I made a turn into the living room hoping to find the wind there, too, but instead this air wasn't breathing. Nothing was. Not even me.

As I looked around the room—the couch, the chairs, the coffee table, the TV—all alone and breathless, my eyes stopped on the old sewing machine. Her father had given it to her.

He had taught her how to sew, and then she taught me.

It looked like a chestnut box with a piano-like top. When opened to 180 degrees, the top rested against the door, which supported it. The machine was lifted from the cavity of the chest, which was filled with fabrics she worked on, making sheets, shirts, pants, dresses.

Suddenly there was noise again.

The stepper was moving slightly up and down, the upright arm was rolling around, and I could hear it all—the rhythmic clicking of her foot as she pressed the pedal, the soft touch she put on clothes as she pushed them under the needle, and her quiet whisper, which sometimes sounded like a prayer and at other times like a lullaby.

"Beth, you have to sing when you sew," she'd declare when I'd watch her.

"I sing all the time," I'd say for the sake of saying something.

"Yes, I know. That's why you don't understand its importance." She'd glance at me, as if to make sure that I was paying attention, and then would turn to her work.

"Singing is fun," I'd challenge her.

"Of course it's fun. It doesn't mean it's not important," she'd respond, not lifting her head, but I'd notice a soft wrinkle on the corner of her lips.

"Mom! What's your point?" I'd ask.

"My point is, fun is a responsibility. Like sewing." She'd smile at me, and I'd see myself in her hazel eyes, in her black hair, in her fair skin, in her red lips, in her determined face, and even in the rhythm of her feet that didn't give up, even when she wasn't paying attention.

I never pushed her beyond that. Never asked her to explain. Now, the machine echoed her very being and I could hear her again, but this time I couldn't ask her for more, though my chest was burning for an answer.

I caught a glimpse of my reflection yet again, this time on the black screen of the TV. My face wasn't pale anymore. All colors seemed brighter. My violet dress looked like a petal from a flower in bloom—faint, yet fresh and blossoming. It was the last thing Mom sewed.

"Promise me you'll wear this."

"I will, mom. Why do you even ask me?"

"Because you change your mind. You like it now, and then in two weeks you don't."

"Mom, I chose the fabric, I am telling you what model I want, why would I change my mind?"

"Beth, it wouldn't be the first time, would it?"

"Mom. I promise. I love it already."

"Yes, yes, of course you do. You sing for fun and you love everything," she said as she started pedaling, and I noticed how she kept a certain rhythm when she would speak, sing, whisper, and even when she was silent.

I put my hands on my shoulders again, tracing the finely sewed lines with my fingers. The smooth feel of the dress made me think of her touch when she measured the length of my back and wrapped the tape around my chest, down my waist, and farther below my hip line. She made the dress exactly like I asked her, not missing a curve, not adding to the length, and keeping the décolleté line where I wanted it, surprising me with her newfound compliance.

I ran my hands down my bosom, my waist, and then felt the deep void in my stomach. All the sewing lines looked like light that glided across me. I remembered her face when she saw me try on the dress for the first time.

"Are you happy?"

I didn't say anything, but I kissed her hands, her cheeks, her eyes, and her hair, and hugged her, feeling her heartbeat on my own chest.

It kept the same rhythm she had kept when she sewed the dress.

The Last Stand by Elison Alcovendaz

I JUST MARRIED a white girl, and nobody cares but my father, the same man who calls himself The Filipino Casanova, which is hard to imagine with his fake teeth and half-burnt face (a chemical attack in a war, he insists).

"She got money?" he asks.

It's that buttery voice, the same one he says would've made him a crooner (or radio personality or game show host) if he'd been born at the right time in the right place with the right skin color. Maybe I can imagine him smooth-talking a woman, but he lives in a storage unit, so where would he take her?

"Her family does," I say.

His taut, stubbly face breaks into a crooked expression of hope, and there he goes, the storyteller, the oral traditionalist, bathing me in his surefire-profit-making proposals as he shuffles around the mostly empty unit like a businessman in a hand-me-down power suit. It's all stuff I've heard before—a chicken fighting ring, a restaurant centered around Auntie Clarita's famous ketchup spaghetti, a professional basketball league for short people only. "Cutting edge" he says more than once, insisting on English, but he tires quickly and sits on the mattress on the floor and lights a cigarette.

"It's not my money," I say.

"I know, *anak*."

Smoke shrouds his face, but the word blasts through like a missile from the war he was never in. This tender word—*child, son*—reeks of desperation on his lips. This man with at least seven kids (that I know of) in at least two other countries with three other women who are not my mother, calls me *anak*.

"Here," I say.

He glances at the bag of weed at his feet and winces, maybe because he knows this is the only reason we see each other—this transaction—but now he's talking again, the academic, the sociologist, a history lesson this time about Filipino obsession with white skin due to colonial rule under Spain and America. He reminds me he has never been with a white woman—their skin so fair you could see your fingerprints dissolve into them—and he's just so impressed with me and my white job, my white house, my white wife, my white life, so impressed. So fucking impressed.

"*Anak*," he says.

But I'm already outside, I'm already in my car, I'm already driving to the suburbs in my Jeep Cherokee, I'm already listening to some guy on NPR talk about something Trump said or didn't say, I'm already hearing my wife talk about the kids on the border as she rolls up her yoga mat, I'm already done, I'm already gone, I'm already here.

Learning English, Teaching Russian by Nina Kossman

THESE BOOKS, HE says and lays his protective hand on the paperback covers, nobody else in this forsaken place is developed enough to comprehend these books, English or no English.

Valery looks up new words in a Russian-English dictionary, which lies on top of his quizzes, and he writes out new words on index cards. When he stands in front of his class, he takes ten or fifteen index cards out of his chest pocket and reads each word aloud so that his privates and privatesses, as he calls his students, would correct his pronunciation of "the aversive no" and "operant conditioning" and "authentic self." He mispronounces English words with so much relish that this ritual grows into a legend that Valery's students tell others—less fortunate ones—whose instructors don't make them privy to their interests in psychology and difficult English words, and who don't make them roll with laughter by mispronouncing "positive reinforcement." It's all because the other instructors have never even heard of the existence of those words. Hey, they're just Russians and there was no psychology in Russia—that's what Valery tells them, and they say that Valery is weird but funny but the other teachers are like dinosaurs from the nineteenth century: man, they don't live in the real world.

Our supervisor doesn't dare question Valery's reading of these books on the job. But one day a supervisor from uphill happens to pass by, and he's never heard of Valery's fame in the downhill departments, and when he says, What an unpleasant surprise it is to see a federal employee immerse himself in extraneous reading matter at tax-payers' expense, Valery says, The government should be honored to support a man like myself while he is mastering the language of his new country and introducing this country's young men and women to the beauty of psychological thought. The uphill supervisor turns to leave because he has nothing to say and he hasn't left quite yet when Valery comments, This is how a big shot leaves when he has nothing to say, and for once I sympathize with a supervisor whose back is so vulnerable. He leaves our room for good, never to come back again.

Zhurkov says, If I were Valery, I wouldn't have bothered coming to work at all, I would've made it clear to said government that it should be even more honored to support me and my love of books in the comfort of my own home. Valery doesn't react to Zhurkov's words, and when we're alone, he explains, Whenever I want to make undeveloped types like Zhurkov shut up, I remember that simply ignoring them does the trick.

But Zhurkov proves this method ineffective and goes back to his teasing. He asks, Do you think Valery missed his vocation? And when I ignore him, he says, Don't you think he should've become an artist? Look at the way he colors pages of those paperbacks—red, blue, green, and look how serious he is about it, how engrossed! An artist manqué, or who knows maybe a something else manqué!

Photo Not Taken by Ruth Knafo Setton

PRELUDE:

We do not deviate an inch from the planned route, do not risk getting off the invisible trolley tracks and finding ourselves "lost in America." Even though Dad has driven this way so many times through the years—and you'd think by now, we could take a chance—some immigrant habits die hard. Like not knowing the names of plants, trees, birds. To me, it's all landscape fleeting past.

Dad and Mom are in the front seat. In the back, my brother Memphis and I sandwich our aunt, Tata Zizou. Mom wears a large straw hat with long red ribbons that flutter over the back of her seat.

Memphis and I are still amazed that when our father, the great adventurer and jazz improviser, gets behind the wheel of an American car in this vast New World, he does not experiment with a single detour. Once he discovered Cape May, New Jersey, he never changed route. Each summer we would drive down the Jersey coast and stay in the same hotel—the enormous Victorian Beach Princess with its thousand tiny windows flickering like a ship at sea. Each evening, we would eat at Tom's Fish Palace.

As we get closer to the beach, I breathe in the fresh, salty air and I'm glad we came. Dad parks where we always do, in front of the shabby, peeling Tom's Fish Palace. Its white stucco grows more dilapidated each year. Not a single car is parked in front.

"Do you think it's still open?" asks Mom.

Tata Zizou says grimly, "If it's not, we have to go back."

I peek in the restaurant's grimy window. "I think I see someone."

Memphis breathes a sigh of relief. "We're saved."

We walk through the musty, wood-paneled dining room to the back deck. We push two tables together, upsetting the faded blue and green umbrella that shades one of them. Moving the tables and chairs as if we're at home, we settle ourselves. Murky depths ripple between the narrow slats of the wood floor. The beauty of it, Dad pointed out when we kids complained that we wanted to go somewhere different, was that we were seated directly above the ocean. Behind the table is a white railing that Memphis and I lean over to see the water. It reminds Dad of cafes in Casablanca, right on the sea.

We order the same thing we always do: fish and chips with Cokes all around. Max, the waiter, is so old and creaky we hate asking him for anything. He hobbles painfully (arthritic knee, which has gotten worse with the years) between the kitchen and us—the only customers. Age spots patch his shaking hands, like the sepia-tinted map of an ancient kingdom.

After we eat, we walk down the tiny boardwalk, a little strip of our childhood. The first year we came, it was sparsely populated. Today, it's nearly abandoned. We pass Taylor Pork Roll (which always sounded disgusting to Memphis and me—a pig rolled up). The arcade, where Memphis and I spent hours testing our skill at Skee-ball and pinball, accumulating long strips of pink tickets for which there were no prizes. We both sighed with boredom through bluegrass concerts held in the "Concert Hall." We used to share soft ice cream cones at the stand next to the arcade. Chocolate for Memphis, vanilla for me, and trading licks so we could taste both. We collected pebbles and shells and set up a store on the beach, where Mom and Dad came to shop. We sat on the rocks, dangling our feet in the water, and played for hours, building elaborate sandcastles with moats, turrets, and dungeons.

As Memphis and I walk along the line of slippery rocks that extends over the ocean—the others far ahead—we reminisce about our yearly stay at the Beach Princess. Every morning we left the hotel carrying blankets, buckets, and shovels. We crossed the street to the line of rocks and walked down the hill to a small stretch of sand where we found, at most, two other families.

On rainy days we played pranks on the guests—most of them old and hard of hearing. Memphis was Emperor of the Elevator, disguised with a black mustache and X-ray glasses, carrying his bag of tricks: sneezing powder, pepper gum, stink bombs, a fake dollar bill attached to a string. We loved Superman comics about the crazy, illogical, upside-down Bizarro world, where beauty was considered ugly. Bizarros did everything backward from those they called "stupid Earth people," and their cracked, blue-lit faces seemed oddly familiar.

THE PHOTO:

Dad, at the wheel of the '57 Chevy. In the front seat, next to him: Mom.

In the back seat: Memphis, Tata Zizou, and me. The car is stopped at the red light in Cape May. Dad has done the unexpected: instead of the traditional route back to the highway, he makes a sudden left turn from the beach and drives through the town of Cape May.

"I hope we won't get lost," worries Zizou.

Memphis and I watch the neatly trimmed gardens, lawns, and brightly painted Victorian houses and inns on either side.

We come to a red light, and I turn my head to the left. "Oh my God!" I let out a cry. "Everyone, look!"

All heads turn. We see a pedestrian-only street opening out from the intersection where we are stopped. A street lined with shops, boutiques, and cafes. It's crowded with tourists in shorts and sunglasses, wearing straw hats, carrying colorful straw bags, eating ice cream cones, and sampling fudge.

Memphis cries, "Look to the right!"

Our heads turn to the right, where the walking street extends. Another block of shops and restaurants. More people surging forth, bustle and action.

The driver behind us blasts his horn. The light has turned green.

A photo of our faces: Tata Zizou sighs, I mutter, "Who knew," Memphis laughs, Mom breathes, "America!" The moment Dad steps on the gas.

That moment.

Pet Rock by Mark Budman

I WALK THE pair of two-year-old identical twins outside my daughter's house. They collect pet rocks, wildflowers, last year's pine needles, and give them to their Deda for safekeeping. *Deda* means grandfather in Russian. *Deda* is me. I'm older than the surrounding hills by a factor of three.

How old are you? I ask one of them.

She brings up her large gray eyes. Two.

And how old am I? Guess.

She struggles. It must be a big number. Four, five, six?

Six, she says.

When I was four, I lived in Siberia.

When I was five, we moved to Kazakhstan.

When I was six, we moved again to Moldova.

Not because we liked to travel, but because Stalin exiled my family. Since then, I've moved a lot, crossing borders and the ocean, finding a new home at least a dozen times.

Now, I interpret for money and pleasure.

The other twin gives me yet another pet rock. It's warm to the touch, and it looks like a miniature meteorite. It's identical to one of its earlier collected sisters. As a meteorite, it traveled far, had time for reflection, and is probably even older than me. By a factor of six.

I collect the girls, and we head home.

Home is where the twins are.

Old Men, No English by Edvin Subašić

EVERY AFTERNOON, I find shade outside Boise High. I sit for hours and chain-smoke. Today is no exception. Teachers complained; "No English!" I said and rolled another one. They went to the principal; I cited religious reasons and stood my ground. Back home, people used to say "smoking like a Turk." Then they shot at anyone related to the Ottomans.

Teachers see me. The security guards see me. My fellow custodians know where I am. They figure I'm too much trouble. They don't know I've already met my quota. I come three hours before everyone. To hell! I can't sleep. Especially in the summer. It's that piercing light in Boise that hovers even at night. In fact, I sleep only in the deep winter, like a bear—or a lazy, snoozing skunk. Cold and snow freeze my thoughts.

Whenever the sun shines, it reminds me that I was a lousy teacher of Total National Defense and history. I taught the kids why the SKS rifle is always better than the AK-47 if they keep at a certain distance. I taught them all the secrets of partisan warfare in case of an invasion by the Soviets or NATO. The Ottomans took our children, I explained. Archduke Ferdinand had to be shot. What the hell was he doing, parading in our streets like that? Did he think he was President Tito? We learned about the past, we talked about foreign invaders. I didn't teach the kids to protect themselves from their neighbors, their family, and their inexperienced hearts filled with desire.

I taught high school in Yugoslavia for twenty-seven years. When I arrived in New York, I got all the shittiest jobs that paid just enough for a meager existence or less, and nobody cared. Six months later, Cousin Ahmed called from Boise. "People here feel bad for refugees," he said. "They'll find you a job that pays enough. Living here is dirt-cheap." One month later, my caseworker in Boise said, "I see you used to teach. I have the perfect job for you."

The maple canopy above my head makes for a perfect place to smoke on September afternoons. I puff on my tobacco for as long as I want. The kids know not to mess with crazy old bastards who don't speak English. When visitors walk by, I scan their gait. There's something about guns that turns men into waddling dicks.

School recently started, and I can see that the rich little turds have already busted out their new toys, parked their shiny cars, and grouped accordingly. I figure half of these kids don't have to worry about money when they grow up—the future CEOs, engineers, professors, and writers. They already know everything. They knew who they were before their umbilical cords were cut. They'll rule the world.

I see that boy, Josh, out there by himself again—a senior who looks like a middle schooler. I wonder if his parents only feed him carrots. I talked to him last Wednesday and told him about today. That cowlick, Mike, is out early on Fridays—no soccer practice. I've seen that shithead making fun of Josh in front of everybody to boost his own little prick.

"This Friday, Josh," I said. "I sit here, you there—" I pointed to a bench near the gym door. "That goose poop, Mike, laughs to you...you hit him. Slap! Like this." I made my palm flat and wide and pressed it to my cheek. "Next, you run here to me."

Oh, I wasn't finished with Mike. A week ago, Mike had come to my bench. "Ci-ga-rette!" he said to me. "One! I give money." He held a dollar in front of my face. I snatched it and grabbed him by his balls. I squeezed until his face went blue and he mouthed for air like a trout. I let him go, and he ran away chasing his own head. He couldn't have known I'd studied pedagogy.

Josh looked at me in disbelief, his pale cheeks two hot burners. "Can't do that, sir. He'll bury me."

"Yes, *can*!" I said. "Why he make fun from you?"

"He didn't used to be like that. We'd been friends since kindergarten."

"Oh, I see. Old comrade. Slap him!" I clapped my hands together. "Listen, son. My student back home…nice kid. When sixteen and he was terrible. I did nothing."

"What happened to him?

"Lost in war." I shrugged and smiled. "Mike…just like him. We do nothing…later he is sociopath, or maybe president."

Josh gave me a long look, as if searching for something invisible on my face, perhaps gauging the extent of bullshit in my story. His eyes were intelligent but danced around nervously.

"Look here!" I pointed to my eyes. "It's good."

It's 3:30, and kids have swarmed the schoolyard. I'm waiting, rolling another cigarette. Josh is at his bench already, reading like always. I notice Mike approaching from the far end, flanked by his cronies and a girl. As if he'd smelled his old friend, Josh looks up from his book, face turning right then left. His eyes meet mine.

Beating Boris by Masha Kisel

EVER SINCE BORIS Efimovich became her stepfather when she was six years old, Sasha fantasized about growing big enough to overpower him. When he smacked the back of her head or hit her arms, buttocks, or stomach with a belt, she imagined him as a frail old man. His white beard down to his knees, he would cower in the corner of their small kitchen as she raised a frying pan over him, ready to beat him senseless.

Four years later, with the help of Hebrew Immigrant Aid Society, they were allowed to leave the Soviet Union. An invisible hand, large as the fear of the unknown, plucked them out of Kiev and carried them from Vienna to Rome to Chicago. They dangled without citizenship, suspended over foreign lands by the kind giant's grasp. At every checkpoint they were interviewed. "How were you persecuted for being Jewish? Which slurs did they call you? Were you beaten? How badly did it hurt and where?"

Boris Efimovich stopped eating. His hair began to grey. His arms grew weak. He could barely manage to slap Sasha across the face.

"Oh, his delicate nerves! Will he make it to 1989?" Sasha's mother cried when they were detained an extra week in Austria.

"Maybe it's because I told them that I'm a good Communist and all Americans are bourgeois pigs?" Sasha said as a joke. No one found it funny. She tried again. "I said that Boris Efimovich is a KGB agent." He was almost too broken to take off his belt. Sasha didn't care. She gorged on Vienna's roasted chestnuts, foot-long hotdogs, and chocolate-covered pretzels. She gaped in amazement at the roses blooming in the middle of December—red as her stepfather's handprint on her cheek—as she walked on a cold beach in Rome.

A few months after they arrived in America, Boris Efimovich stopped leaving their fourth-story Chicago apartment. All day long he sat in an armchair they had salvaged from the dumpster, watching the empty yard—so different from their neighborhood in Kiev. There were no gossiping grandmothers warming benches, no children playing outside.

"This is America?" he'd say in a frightened whisper. "Where are all the people?"

Sasha bundled up in a coat too small for her rapidly growing body and walked out the door. She was meeting her new friend Amy at the Greek diner where they would eat American French fries and laugh in English. Sasha looked up.

Boris Efimovich was just a small figure in the window.

She Is a Battleground by Nancy Au

TWELVE-YEAR-OLD BUTTER BOYS face the old Chinese woman they call Baboochka. Imagine: the eighty-year-old woman on their apartment's shared front stoop, the silver moon caught in her tousled hair, her yellow sweater vest, her milky-white Velcro E-Z Steppers. She jostles grocery bags from one hip to the other as she digs in her pockets for keys. She grumbles about the checker at the vegetable market pocketing her change, about her arthritic fingers too weak to open jars but too strong for the wet lettuce bag, about the bus driver that did not hear her call out for a stop. And now, the butter boys on her stoop who whistle for sesame candy, beg to see inside her bags, throw dirty leaves in her hair when she refuses.

The old woman knows that in two years the boys will become teenage fools: lanky legs, smelly, soiled underpants, an erection when someone taps their shoulder or sloshes in a puddle or fires a gun. It doesn't take much. The fools will come home from school and find the old woman weaving long green blades of grass into her house slippers like laces, her purse filled with acorns, resting against her stockinged feet. The fools will laugh and point their sticky fingers at Baboochka, so close they leave fingerprints on her eyeglasses.

And the old woman will choose to fight back. In her own true myth, she is not a corny grandmother, soft like a pillow. She is not Mother Dear. She is not Lady Khorosho, just waiting to become a ghost. She does not weep and cry and mumble. No.

She is a battleground. *Lui yun* is her real name, she will tell the fools. Go and *puk gai*. She is a person. She is sex. She is useful poison. She is a survivor of wars. She is a dream. She is a sarcastic beast. She is the skeleton key who understands little criminals. She will yank the fools' earlobes with joy, grab handfuls of shirt and rip them a new hemline.

And the arrogant snots will call her mad, crazy, a shit-head, a starry buttock, a whore. But the old woman will laugh and laugh, howl like a *bolshy* dame. The sound—quick, scratching—the sweetest noise you've ever heard. Like an ancient drug, with chipped teeth like tin bells, a tongue like a rake, a fighting drive to live, a horror heart in woolly slippers.

Mushrooms by Irina Popescu

THE MOTHER SHOWS her daughter where she stores the two pieces of jewelry she owns. When the daughter is fifteen, the mother tells her they are war heirlooms.

Heirloom sounds like mushroom and those grew everywhere there. To pick them is to know the difference between life and death.

When the daughter is sixteen, the mother gives her instructions: When I die, go to my sock drawer, get the key. It's tucked into the only black socks I own. Open the oak drawer. Listen to me one last time. Her mother gives her these instructions every year, in the same tone, with the same determination.

I don't want to talk about this, Mama, the daughter says each time. Thoughts of her mother dying are too strong. In fact, she hardly ever thinks of dying, the word too marked by finality. Since they left home the daughter never really found a place to exist again. She roamed around new people and learned a new language, but that was not enough to exist.

One day her mother dies in a country that is not her own. The daughter is twenty-two and not ready to lose her mother, as daughters are never ready to lose their mothers. The daughter goes to the sock drawer. She finds the black socks. Her slight fingers tickle the key out. She goes to the locked oak drawer in her mother's closet and opens it. She finds the heirlooms, an oval golden locket with one petite amber stone pressed in its center and two ivory drop earrings. Inside the locket she finds a folded piece of yellow paper. It has an address, a key, and some words on it. She reads them. She also finds an envelope with money. Money saved, somehow.

The daughter follows the instructions and listens. She packs a handful of clothes she had left at home into her mother's flannel suitcase. She packs her mother's ashes safely into the middle of the suitcase, lays the earrings and locket next to them. She gets into her mother's injured Volvo and drives to the airport. She buys a ticket and waits. When she arrives, she knocks even though this was her mother's house. No one is home because this was her mother's house.

She looks around the yard, her eyes tracing the forest rising beyond the back porch. This yellow house with the petite deck that the two of them stained with the juice of fresh raspberries before moving to America. Art, her mother had said.

Mushrooms grew everywhere then, and still do. The daughter picks a few off a wet tree trunk and realizes she can't remember a life without her mother in it. Frothy poison ivy surrounds dozens of ticklish insects crawling on tall blades of yellowing grass, which surround the underbelly of what her mother had said were the best mushrooms for three-egg omelets and cheese quiches.

Walking around the back porch, she gently slides the key into the lock and opens the back door. The kitchen looks dark yet still somewhat cheerful. A faint smell of flour and dust mites arises. She imagines her mother's hands rolling out flakey homemade pie crusts after work. She hasn't been home in years, she thinks, as she traces her fingers across the dirty kitchen sink where her mother taught her to never wash mushrooms. They come from the earth and the bits of dirt engrained on their skin allow our bodies to return to that earth, she remembers her mother's echoing words. The concept of home disturbs her. Her identity makes no sense without her mother's reminders of this place and of the language they share. Shared.

She grabs her suitcase and goes into her old bedroom. She unpacks her mother's ashes. She puts on the golden locket with one petite amber stone pressed in its center and the two ivory drop earrings and heads out to the back yard. She thinks of that Sylvia Plath poem about inheriting the earth. She sprinkles ashes here and there, watching the wind pick some up and twirl them around the contours of her body.

Years later she will return to this place, this home no longer home, to pick mushrooms with her daughter in the forest behind her mother's house where the mushrooms spring into bloom, outlining the contours of their inherited bodies.

PART FOUR

Tired of waiting for home

Acknowledgements by Alexandros Plasatis

It was night when we were flying from Birmingham to Shanghai, and I was watching films. At some point I felt an impulse to look outside, and so I did. For the first time since we took off I looked outside and down there I saw the lights of a night town. I glanced at the screen with the map of the airplane's route: we were flying above Kavala, my hometown.

The 24/7 café by the harbour where I had grown up working, the broken-down ice machine, the great big sun, the customers sitting in the shade of the lime trees, their fingers tapping on the tables. The sky that was blue and the sea that was bluer, and the island opposite that was dark, dark green, and that girl, the night-girl with the shadows in her eyes who wanted her cappuccino with lots and lots of sprinkles. All those small, chipped, round trays, and the other tray—the massive one, the tray that no one but me could master—always propped against the wobbling stool of my waitering days and nights from where I saw it all—everything might still be there.

I returned to watch the end of the film, then went for a piss.

Two Nights Only by Philip Charter

IT WAS HOT and I was killing time walking the streets of some terracotta-brick town in Mexico. I was on my own, on vacation from the other terracotta-brick town where I lived. My contract still had three months to run, so I thought I may as well see a different place, but it was mostly the same.

I heard a truck behind me, rumbling along in the traffic crawl with its loudspeaker message blaring. "*The circus is coming for two nights only!*" I removed my headphones to listen better. There would be clowns, acrobats, children's characters—the usual.

When the truck passed, I saw thick bars and a metal roof bolted onto the flatbed. Inside the makeshift cage was a tiger: an actual, fully-grown, tiger. I stopped walking and stared.

The animal was spread on the floor like a pancake, head on its paws, displaying its size but none of its power or menace. It wasn't a great advert for the circus. Perhaps it was carsick. It certainly wasn't pacing up and down, snarling through the bars as you might expect. It looked out and I looked in—two foreigners locking eyes. Was this what I came to see, a dying version of old Mexico? If I went to the circus, would I see animals corralled by moustached men in red coats and top hats?

The traffic lurched forward, and the truck disappeared around the next corner. Before I knew what was happening,

I was running after it. I desperately needed another look. As I rounded the corner onto the next street, I spotted the truck at the end of the block, waiting at a junction in the hundred-degree heat. The truck crossed the junction and carried on. I wasn't sure if I would ever see it again.

As I ran, I dodged the fruit stands and telephone poles positioned in the middle of the sidewalk. The tiger remained tantalisingly out of reach around forty yards ahead. I chased the thing for eight blocks, tracking its distance by its loud-speaker advertisement. I clamped my hand to my shoulder bag to stop it from bouncing around as I ran. The traffic slowed, and I finally gained ground. The car in front was held at a red light.

When I came alongside it, I was panting and sweat poured from every part of me. My t-shirt clung to my back like a baby to its mother. I reached into my bag and dug out my camera before the lights could change. I lifted my head and looked at the beast. It didn't move; it just stared at me with empty eyes like it was in a holding pattern, tired of waiting for home. I didn't know who was more disappointed, the tiger or me. What good was it being so powerful if all you saw through the bars of your cage was another animal trapped?

I fanned myself with my cap, unsure if I was even going to take the picture. Then, the lights changed and the truck moved off, kicking up dust.

I lowered my camera.

"*The circus is coming for two nights only!*" The sound of the advertisement faded to quiet, then the truck turned right, and it was gone.

Crayfish Cocktail by Stuart Stromin

My FATHER WAS a gambler and in the hot South African summer of my eleventh year, when Hendrik Verwoerd was Prime Minister, I used to caddy for him, the Greek giant, the man with the beard, the two Indians, and the custard face, serving drinks and fetching cigarettes from Rodray's café while they played poker on hot Wednesday and Sunday afternoons. I loved standing at my father's side in the cool dark room at the back of our house, watching the bright rectangular chips clatter like gemstones into the center of the green tablecloth. The varying shades and shapes of the faces around the table formed a perfect foil for the pile of riches heaped up on the baize. Running errands to the liquor cabinet and back was a small price to pay for entrance to the magic show that these games were for me.

Sometimes, when the pile grew really big, like a huge coral island in the middle of a green tropical sea, my father would send me out of the room. On one of those days, he told me to see if Rodray sold smelling salts in his café, and all the men laughed loudly (except for the custard face, who never spoke a word). When I came back from Rodray's empty-handed, the custard face and the beard were gone. I never saw them again. The two Indians were giggling to themselves and shaking their heads; the big Greek was pouring himself a drink, which must have been sour or something, judging from the way his face twisted as he drank it. My father was smiling and called me over to him.

I was too old to sit on his knee, but he picked me up, nevertheless, and looked me right in the eyes. "Son," he said solemnly, "never play the game too long." Then he squeezed a purple five-rand note into my hand and said, "Be lucky."

That night, we all went out to dinner at a fancy hotel in Johannesburg. I had crayfish cocktail, cream of mushroom soup, rump steak medium rare, and vanilla ice cream for dessert.

My older brother and my married sister were there as well. I saw my father give my brother a pile of money as thick as old yellow newspapers, and when my brother asked, "Royal flush?" my father just laughed and laughed until tears came from his eyes. Even I was allowed a sip of wine that night and on the way home everyone was joking and singing.

I was the first person to notice that the front window of our house had been smashed. When we went inside, we found that all our things had been stolen. The house was a mess. "Blacks," said my father, but my mother just looked at him with narrowed eyes saying, "Oh, y-e-e-e-s," as if she was singing the note of a song.

They sent me straight to bed, but I could not sleep. I could hear them shouting at each other until late into the night. Then I heard the front door slam, and I knew in the darkness of my bedroom that my father was going out to find the people who had broken into our home.

I dreamed that night that playing cards were real kings and queens living in a palace in downtown Johannesburg. I woke to hear my mother sobbing and then there were policemen in our house who looked as if they never slept and people in pajamas who looked as if they had not woken up. My married sister came from Pretoria to fetch us.

Years afterward, I learned that the Murder and Robbery Squad had arrested the two Indians almost immediately, but they had apparently released them after two days in custody. A real solution to my father's death, a senior police officer told me, would have been impossible. Nothing could be proved against any of the players, and the case was officially closed only ten days after the murder.

Today, I never gamble, but I must admit that the fascination for the tumbling kings and queens of Bicycle has never left me.

Every time I look back on my youth, or on my father, I remember—not the final image of my father bleeding outside our house—but the purple five-rand note pressed on my palm and the archipelago of stars on an emerald sky, which delighted me in the magic show of my childhood.

The Wake by Rimma Kranet

HE WAS CURSING at me as I stood swaying the baby on the side of my hip.

My hip bone was protruding under the weight of our child, her legs dangling like chains from an abandoned swing, restless, relentless.

He cursed from the kitchen, and through the open door he hurled his words, strong and free, into the stale air.

He raised his voice, eyes bulging in anger. His face looked fleshy and square, cheekbones dissipating under the fatty skin, his chin a sliver of a new moon.

I had undone the evening meal. The clams in the big silver pot, which were supposed to have been briefly immersed in boiling water, had instead completely opened up their waterlogged shells and emptied their precious cargo into the salty water, resulting in the probability of an imperfect plate of pasta with clams.

I had downplayed the importance of timing.

The small kitchen filled with steam and the odor of the sea permeated everything.

"Why is this so important to you?' I asked already knowing the answer.

"Because we do not eat like pigs," he said.

"Who cares about the clams..." I argued.

"You should have stayed at home with the baby. You shouldn't have come," he said.

"What? Are you going to yell at me because of the clams? Are you going to insult me over a plate of spaghetti with clams?" I insisted.

"Shut up," I heard, and then silence.

His face was so close to mine that I had to take a step back to focus.

We had driven for seven hours in the dark to be here. In this kitchen. In this house where everything was familiar to me, yet nothing was dear. I insisted on coming; I thought it would be easier than having to take a bus at the last minute if he decided to fall apart.

"Take the baby and wait in the bedroom," he said.

His father was dead. My father-in-law was dead. My in-law was dead. That seemed more accurate, for he had never been anything remotely like a father to me.

He lay in his casket, fully dressed in the suit he wore to our wedding—his only good, dark suit. Rigid, starched like his white shirt, his silk tie aligned perfectly down the middle of his body, as though dividing the good from the bad. His face gaunt from weeks of barely eating, his will imposed on those who cared for him and about him.

He lay at an angle, naturally inclined toward the gaze of those who came to bid him farewell for the last time, his feet facing the open door. His hands formed fists as they lay at his sides. There was much hovering and whispering and swaying back and forth on the simple chairs that formed a closed circle around him, as though around a campfire.

The lampshades were strewn with gauzy red scarves basking the room in a rose-colored haze, making it seem like the walls were blushing.

I peered into the crowded room of mourners on my way to the bedroom where I had been ordered to go.

"Touch him...see how cold he is. Touch him, don't be afraid..." Someone reached for my arm to pull me closer.

"I don't want to..." I said, "I'm not afraid...I just don't like it..."

There was a hum coming from the crowd reciting the rosary. The women were all dressed in black. It was hard to tell them apart, as if they had assumed a common identity. Under their black scarves, their faces blended into one.

Their fingers worked diligently as they rubbed the smooth beads in unison. Heads lowered into their laps, they consoled themselves with the words of God. Some had been there all day carrying out their duty. They had such an intimate familiarity with death. These days, the town's church bells only rang for funerals or daily mass. I had learned to tell the difference. The "Mother Church" was just a few cobblestoned blocks away.

I spent my summers in this house. In this tiny village on top of a mountain, surrounded by a forest I have never seen.

In the evenings during the month of July I sat in the living room on a brown wooden chair and leaned into the feeble sound of the television set that stood facing me. It was an old set—square and heavy, thick and grey. So as not to disturb the silence, I sat in the dark. The picture illuminated my skin, smooth and tan from countless hours spent lounging by the sea watching my children play.

Once in a while a distant echo of voices coming from the local café reached me. There were moments of abrupt laughter, shouting, the hollow sound of feet running through the empty square outside our windows.

During the day it was hot and there were tiny insects that descended upon you as you sat under the inviting shade of the trees. There was nothing to do but hope that someone would drive you the ten kilometers of winding road it took to get to the beach.

My husband watched me from the kitchen doorway as I stood on the brink of moving past the women in mourning. Past all of his aunts and cousins, past his nieces, childhood friends and old lovers who had outgrown their age. They looked earnest, lost in their prayer books as if pleading for time.

There was a Madonna and Child with an electric candle burning beside it on the far end of the room.

I could feel my daughter's warmth against me and it reminded me that I was an intruder, a spectator on my way to somewhere else.

Welcome the Red Army by Walerian Domanski

THE VILLAGE OF Zagonowo, located in the province of Silesia in Poland, split into two camps. Some peasants felt that when the Red Army entered the village, there should be a welcome ceremony with bread and salt on a tray as a traditional Polish symbol of hospitality, as well as the red flag. Elder Wojtal, especially, supported the idea of a welcome ceremony. But the majority of the peasants thought it would be best to stay out of sight in their houses as the Red Army passed through the village.

"Let the Russians know that we are not Germans from Silesia, but Poles from Silesia and we should give them warm welcome," argued Wojtal.

However, most of the peasants thought that the safer path would be to wait and see.

"The quieter you are on the journey, the longer distance you will travel," explained Janik.

"What happens if the Germans win the war and then return to our village?"

"It is a stupid question! They will shoot us immediately at the fence."

"They will not be back! The Germans are finished!" argued Wojtal.

After a lengthy discussion, the difficult decision was made that the Red Army was to be welcomed by a delegation of all the Communists living in the village. It turned out that there were only three Communists: Wojtal, Basior, and Kupczyk. Each man did not own any land and they were all very poor.

"We should add a bottle of strong homemade whiskey to the bread and salt," advised Basior, who was also known as the village drunkard.

"It is a good idea; Russians like to drink," confirmed Wojtal.

"What about the translation? How will we communicate with Russians?" asked Kupczyk.

"The Russian soldiers know the Polish language because, after all, the Russians occupied Poland before 1918 and again after 1939."

Bread, salt, and a bottle of strong moonshine whiskey were prepared in a nearby kitchen. After a long search, a nice tray and red flag were found. All that remained was to write a short speech, which took a lot of time. The speech was written on a sheet of paper torn from a school notebook. Wojtal placed it in his pocket.

Now there was nothing to do but wait for the arrival of the Russians. As they waited, the peasants of the village Zagonovo did not waste time. It was a sunny and warm day; they sat down on the grass and talked about politics. They wondered what kind of Poland would exist in the future, without the Germans' occupation. There was uncertainty and even pessimism. Only Wojtal, Kupczyk, and Basior were happy and full of optimism. The debate was spirited, especially since the discussion was not held with dry mouths—as could be expected with peasants waiting for the Red Army.

After two hours had passed, the muffled roar of engines could be heard in the distance.

"Tanks, tanks!" someone shouted.

Wojtal, Basior, and Kupczyk ran to the edge of the village. The roar became louder, and then the tanks grew visible as they approached the village. The delegation went on the road as the tanks approached. On the first tank waved a red flag with the hammer and sickle. A similar red flag, but without the hammer and sickle, fluttered in Wojtal's hand. He wept with joy and pride.

Fearfully, the rest of the villagers watched from their hiding places. Even the children, curious as they were, kept their distance. The first tank stopped before the three-man delegation. The others halted in succession.

The commander of the first tank was dirty and dusty. He removed his helmet to reveal curly hair and a tawny complexion. He was Asian, short and stocky, very possibly Kazakh or Uzbek. His face looked tired. He leaped down onto the road. As he walked over to the peasants, he saw the tray with the bottle and smiled. The peasants smiled in return.

"We welcome the Red Army," announced Wojtal, holding out the tray to the commander. Without answering, the commander grasped the bottle and opened it with a blow of his hand on the bottom. The peasants relaxed, and a few emerged gingerly from their hiding places to watch what was happening down the road. The commander tilted the bottle and began to drink. Suddenly, to the astonishment of the delegation, he spat, and threw the bottle down onto the sandy road. He pulled his pistol from its holster and shot straight at Wojtal's forehead. Wojtal slumped to the road.

"Sun of the beech!" shouted the commander.

He jumped onto his tank, leaving the peasants standing by the side of the road frozen with fear.

"Drive!" he shouted as he gave the signal for the line of tanks to follow him.

The tanks left the village in a cloud of dust. The remaining—now two-man—delegation stood motionless.

The first to regain his senses was Basior. He picked up the bottle from the ground and took a drink. Then, like the commander, he spat out the contents.

"It is water!" he shouted.

"Someone drank the whiskey and replaced it with water," said Kupczyk.

"Or someone exchanged the bottles—bourgeois sabotage!" yelled Basior.

Basior bent over Wojtal. "Wojtal, are you alive? Wojtal, say something." After a moment he told Kupczyk with resignation, "He is dead."

Kupczyk, pale as a wall, was running helplessly in place.

The peasants ran to the scene at the edge of the village, but Wojtal could not see them. He lay still in the road, a look of astonishment frozen on his face. Around his head, the stream of blood had grown to a small puddle. Beside him lay a red flag covered with dust. Fields of grain swayed gently in the breeze, as if venerating the dead.

Disbelief by A. Molotkov

For A.K. Kazansky

HE'D TALKED ABOUT it for more than a year, but I didn't believe him. Who would? Would you believe it if someone told you they could dissolve in water? The first time, he added hastily, Please, don't laugh—but I laughed anyway; I'd already started. At first, I thought he was kidding, but how many times do you repeat a joke? Then I assumed he enjoyed the strangeness of it. I didn't argue, and he'd give me this look—now I know what it meant. After seven years together, he must have hoped I would believe him without reservations.

That night, when he said he was ready to dissolve, I was annoyed by this new twist in our game. I'd come to resent him for overdoing this dissolution warning act, the unorthodox ritual of it. I asked whether he was going to dissolve permanently; he didn't know—it took time to feel how ruthless this answer was. He said nothing else, made no farewell gestures. I was in bed, waiting for him. He took forever. I got bored and called out. No reply. The tub was full, and I knew right away but pretended not to. I looked all around the house—nothing. Could he have slipped out without my noticing? Impossible, considering where I sat in bed, with a full view of both the bathroom and the bedroom doors.

A year passed. I had to face it: he wasn't coming back. He wouldn't keep me in the dark for so long. Or would he, for my disbelief? What if he lived in another town, enjoying every day of his new life? I pushed these thoughts away—they revealed that I still didn't believe him. My betrayal was ongoing.

I kept the water in the bathtub for some time. It was just water and its appearance hadn't changed, but I knew it would eventually evaporate. I had to let it go. I couldn't leave him in time's hands. I pulled the plug and watched the water drain and absurdly, I felt he was also watching, right there in the bathroom. He was smiling. He'd forgiven me. I knew that if he could, he would hold me close and stroke my head.

So, was it suicide or merely a transformation into a state unknown to most of us? I hope he didn't do it out of despair. I'm sure he had already forgiven me back then, when the two of us—the real I, the imaginary he—watched the unnecessary water disappear. Perhaps he'd forgiven me from the start. From that first time he mentioned it, knowing I would laugh, not expecting me to believe?

The Immaculate Heart of Mary by Ingrid Jendrzejewski

STEEL CITY, 1910

Magda descends on Polish Hill like so much of the metal whose siren song lured our fathers and grandfathers away from their *matki* and motherland. Within a week, she is selling newspapers on the street corners. Within two, she has us organized. We wear our brothers' clothing; we cut our hair. She teaches us to spit; we forget our breasts. She brings us papers; we sell them. We take our pennies; she takes a cut.

At first, we are ecstatic: we can now turn paper into copper into bread. Our fathers may wring coins from steel, but their kind of money is passed to the old country, evaporating like our memories of the words of the *Bogurodzica*.

But then things start to shift. One by one, we feel a dent, notice a hollow. We begin to feel a missing. When we walk, our chests crackle.

And sure enough, when we look, we find that our hearts are gone. Our chests are filled with crumpled newsprint. We float when we walk because there is nothing to weigh us down, but it is a lightness that makes us feel heavy.

Magda lives near the *Kosciół Matki Boskiej*, and when I pass it, I hear the blood beat through its domes. I make the sign of the cross. She is not at home when I arrive, but there is no lock on the door, and I let myself in.

Her room is small, so I see them immediately: our hearts are wrapped in newspaper, lined up in rows along the floorboards. I look for mine, but it is not with the others. I find it elsewhere, near her pillow, in her bed. It looks as if it has been used.

I want to seize it, free it, take back what is mine. But when my hand brushes Magda's sheets, I find myself unable to move. There are nickels in my pockets, and I am thinking about love.

I will stand here until Magda returns, until I am sure of my own mind. I will stand here while the bells of the Immaculate Heart of Mary ring in the eventide, until the blood in my veins is black and thick like ink.

The Ghosts of Other Immigrants by Maija Mäkinen

On that last night at the corner bar, she says she likes to listen to a) Frank Sinatra and b) Ingrid Caven singing French chansons in German, not necessarily in that order.

Oooh, that voice, Ingrid *Caven*!

Her own voice squeaks with excitement and she looks askance in coy horror. It was a beautiful cabaret voice once, hers, she says with a theatrical bend of the wrist, and purses her rose lips around the cocktail straw.

Latvian, eighty-five (she let it slip), with painted-on eyebrows, a powdered face, and whippoorwill hair under a black beret, it's all softness about her—the silk bow at her throat, the elegant fabrics, the frothy highballs with forgotten names. It's unclear what *hers* is—Dagnica, Dana, Leigh—she claims them all, and the professions of actress, call girl, singer.

Her gestures are a comedy of manners, and she tells stories of high drama, of the singing career, before her voice was ruined, of nights in New York, of lovers, of women and men.

She is losing her friends and her memories, and we remind her of her preferred ones, to let her shine. She knows: a shrewd appreciation in her eyes.

Tell us about Latvia when you were little.

She laughs a stage laugh, though it tinkles.

The parties, oh! and the Latvian traditions! The porch, and the cherry trees…my mother, she had such deep kind of carpenting, so pale, I don't know how she kept those carpets clean.

Dagnica/Dana/Leigh, confusing carpentry for carpeting, in the house the Russians stole, so many decades ago.

I had a white dress...

When you were little? I ask, imagining a flapper frock and an oversized bow on her head.

...you don't need a house, they said to me. They gave it to my brother and gave me two thousand dollars. *You'll get married*, they said. But I never did.

You mean the house in Latvia?

In New *Jersey*! I had to get out, I was under terrible stress, and he stole everything, all the porcelain and the lace.

I thought it was the Russians who stole—

An angry pivot of her head. Her eyes glitter cold.

Those damn Russians!

Oh, no, tell us about the men, about love.

Oh! There were so many, artists, you know, painters, handsome, they painted pictures of me, so many, all over the walls.

I had once visited her Ninth Street tenement, where we sat in her kitchen drinking green highballs while a rat emerged from behind the refrigerator. She had measured me: would I scream—I dare you, her eyes said. I didn't, nodded only and drank the sweet liquor and picked up my bag as the rat bustled, unconcerned by our presence.

We shared a jar of Swedish herring and Russian black bread, even though the Swedes had once owned Finland and the Russians us both. Afterwards she led me through her two runty rooms: in the first a twin-sized bed of cloudy linens and ruched satin pillows, in the second a bay window coated with decades of dust. In the filtered light, the walls of the room sighed with fading portraits of a nude with easy contours. Bare young flesh in oil, watercolor, and Kodak, just as she had told us, rendered by artists content to replicate her perfect breasts with little heed to the complications of their subject. Otto Dix or Alice Neel might have perceived more, but they hadn't come knocking.

Now, the beret slips. She's on her second cocktail.

Tell us about the teleprompters, someone says.

Oh, the teleprompters, they call me all the time, every day, trying to sell me things!

Her voice shrills, gets away from her, and she sighs.

I was going to the burial.

Oh, did someone die?

...he was an Italian, they put him on that island with the prisoners; it's on the subway map. No, you can't go, the woman says to me – there's no funeral for destitutes. She said he was a destitute.

She's talking about the potter's field on Hart Island, run by Rikers inmates. She rounds her eyes as if to focus.

I have cadillacs, in my eyes.

Cataracts?

Yes, like I said!

The corners of her mouth turn down, and like a child in a grown-up's chair, she treads her feet in the air.

You should fix your hair nicer, she says to me, the way my grandmother in Finland used to, and digs out her money purse. She's had her fill of gimlets and us.

Better leave in fair weather, she says.

Better leave before her bowlegs fail again on Second Avenue and leave her leaning on a lamp post in the rain.

Good night, she says, is helped down from her stool.

See you soon, I say.

She kisses me on the mouth, a powdery taunt.

Maybe you will, she says, her eyes in flinty slits, and maybe you won't, and I think that in a few short decades this will be me, this shrunken woman bent over her cane, a long way from home.

Searching for Elsewheres that Lead to Somewheres by Kathy Nguyen

THÚY MUSED HOW Buddha's lotus altar table lights never protected her family from the shadows that haunted them. Her husband always believed shadows of his war-torn past made it difficult for him to restart his life as a human. He died before he could truly feel like a human.

This morning marked the forty-ninth day since her husband's death. His Buddhist burial should be scheduled for today, but it wasn't. They never had a proper discussion about their funeral arrangements. While it was difficult to predict death, there was no way to escape it when its time came.

The only time he talked about his potential death was during the war. After witnessing so many deaths, he predicted he would die in battle somewhere. War meant to kill or be killed. So he believed what his comrades told him: their bodies would disappear and become forgotten as the war became a memory.

That didn't happen. Instead, surgery to repair a ruptured abdominal aortic aneurysm caused his organs to fail. He couldn't fight with a dying body, and months after his hospitalization, his life became a pile of delicate ashes sealed in a Ziploc bag.

Years ago, Thúy imagined that their bodies would be buried, becoming one with Mother Nature, but their children decided to have their father's body cremated. They wouldn't allow it to further decay by natural elements or be devoured by organisms that lived underneath the earth. Their children never asked her what she wanted, but she never complained. She had a family who would respect her dead body. Her mind never stopped imagining what happened to those who died during the war. Those bodies that became forever lost, misplaced in their homeland.

Questions about what to do with her husband's ashes turned into arguments. After a brief reunion via international phone calls, her husband's surviving family in Việt Nam requested his ashes be returned to them. Her husband's family didn't want his spirit wandering a country that never welcomed him. He fought for his motherland; he should be buried in her soil.

"*Families can reconnect after death,*" a static voice told her over the phone.

"*But death means distance. So, home can be anywhere,*" Thúy quietly responded.

Her children voiced their disagreement. In their eyes, family meant proximity. A burial plot was to be purchased at one of the many memorial gardens here; they promised Thúy that they would visit their father's grave during the holidays, his birthday, and his death anniversary. Their idea of home was where they were physically settled and living in the present. His body needed to remain with his immediate family.

Home was singular. People like Thúy and her husband weren't allowed to have two homes in two countries. Home indicated one's allegiance.

It was exasperating when both families were connected and disconnected by that perilous strand of distance.

Instead of burning two sticks of sandalwood incense for her husband and Quan Âm, the bodhisattva of compassion, she found herself taking her husband's urn and driving off to a nearby river in the cold spring morning. The windburn didn't discourage her. She walked closer to the river, hoping to hear the sounds of the water's gentle stream. She remembered listening to the changing sounds of the ocean's turbulent water as the boat sailed away from Việt Nam's chaos. That was forty-two years ago, a time when hundreds or even thousands of people were crammed into a boat as they fled from home. Back then, people were occupied with the water's currents. If the water was kind to them, they would survive.

Now, the river brought back memories of how bodies crowded that boat. She remembered how there were no spaces between them. She remembered that her husband would never sleep, observing how the movements of the ocean's waves escorted them to survival. There were no maps; they had to trust the water.

She breathed in the cold air and turned to walk back to her car. She would drive back home—but instead, she opened the passenger door and stared at her husband's urn.

Maybe this was her intent from the beginning.

His death had become a matter of where home was. They both shared a strong desire to return to Việt Nam, but their years living here—in anger and guilt—were equally strong. All that weight of conflicting tensions had become too heavy for them to balance. Home was nowhere now.

She threw the urn into the river, feeling the rush of everything, and nothing, as it floated in the direction of where the water would lead it. The urn would drown somewhere, and over time, her husband's ashes would scatter themselves across the river. Thúy hoped he would forgive her for continuing his displacement in this unremarkable river, where waves and tides moved without a clear destination in mind.

But she believed that, like migratory people, water constantly traveled in different directions. Something about his ashes migrating through the river—perhaps through the ocean—in search of a new home seemed fitting to her. There was a time when they were struggling to move, fighting the unforgiving rhythm of the ocean's water to relocate to another elsewhere that would welcome them. There were multiple relocations and elsewheres.

She wanted to believe that his ashes would return to somewhere, even if that meant not here or there. And she could only hope that the gentle and sometimes harsh waves of this foggy water would steer him to a peaceful somewhere in his afterlife. Because their home was located somewhere between those moving waves.

Hilsa in Hog Plum Sauce by Sayantika Mandal

I

Black clouds hovered in the sky clamoring for war, flashing swords of lightning to the battle-drum of thunder. The wind blew gusts of rain, and the children hurried to shut the wooden window, which rattled like a chained monster.

The mother was worried. No vendors had come to sell vegetables. The rains poured down in sheets, and no one dared to venture out. She checked the little space in the corner of the kitchen. A few potatoes and some shriveled hog plums stared back from the cane baskets. She did not want to worry the father, who pored over a book in his study, sipping a cup of chai. Should she boil rice and lentils together? She checked the tin that stored lentils. It would not be enough for her brood of eight children. Nine soon; she caressed her little bulge and smiled.

Somebody banged on the wooden door. She hurried to open it. The fishmonger woman came in, drenched in rain and shivering, her eyes gleaming. Her silver nose ring dripped water; she took the huge cane basket covered with a dirty cloth down from her head.

"Got a great catch of hilsa. The river has flooded, and they were swimming in the paddy fields. Only fifteen rupees. I'll cut and clean it for you."

The mother whispered a prayer as she went inside to bring money from the box she kept in the niche carved on her bedroom wall. Thick slices of hilsa flaming in their own amber fat—her children would love them with a steaming plate of rice.

The coals were hot in her earthen oven, and she fanned the flames. The fillets slid down into the wok; yellow mustard oil sputtered, droplets leaping up and scalding her arm. Her gold bangles jingled as she jerked her arm and moved away to check for blisters. And then, she saw the hog plums.

She called her eldest daughter in. The girl was seventeen and quiet. She asked her to crush the hog plums with a little water. When the fish was fried, she set it aside and kneeled on the floor to wet-grind mustard seeds on the stone slab.

She simmered the hog plums in the mustard paste, added the hilsa, and covered it with a plate. The flavors of the fish mingled with the tartness of the hog plums and the pungent mustard paste. She served each child a slice of hilsa and a spoonful of the sauce, and they smacked their lips in delight and asked for more gravy.

She ate last of all, the tail-end of the fish, the only part left. After she put away the plates, she went for her afternoon siesta. The rain pattered on.

A year later, the eldest daughter, married and pregnant, lived in a state where there were no rivers teeming with fish. She craved hilsa and hog plum, but none were to be found.

II

She is going to be late for work; it is past eight. Dark clouds menace the sky, but she can't afford to lose another paid holiday. She scans the market, where fishmongers exhibit their catch on a blue tarp. They weigh and cut the fish into pieces with huge fish-knives and haggle with the customers as they hand over the fillets in smelly plastic bags. Stray cats mewl around, chewing blood-soaked innards of the fish that have been discarded.

"Fresh hilsa! Five hundred rupees a kilo."

Both of her daughters love hilsa in hog plum sauce, and there are hog plums in the pantry. If she can have the maid fry the fillets and crush the plums while she showers, she could cook it and still make it to the office in time.

She doesn't bargain with the fishmonger. She hands over a five-hundred rupee note and marches home.

"Wash the fish and fry them with mustard oil. Lightly, not too much. Crush the hog plums in water. Fast," she tells the maid as she hands her the bag.

Ten minutes later, her hair wrapped in a towel, she goes to the kitchen and switches on the vent. No matter how many times she tells the maid, she never switches it on. But there is no time to tell her off. There is no mustard paste in the fridge, and she asks her to wet-grind some in the grinder. She turns the gas knob on; the oil on the iron wok is hot, smelling of the hilsa. She still uses an iron wok, like her mother did, and not those Teflon-coated ones. Dried red chilies and spices sputter on the oil. The sound of rain outside is drowned out by the whirring machines in the kitchen.

It is almost nine. The fish simmers in the hog plum gravy, little bubbles rising to the surface. "Cover and cook for a few more minutes," she tells the maid. "Serve it when they come back from school." She scampers out of the house, umbrella in one hand and her bag in the other, into the muddy street to take the bus, knowing her daughters will not complain about the food today.

III

She will fly to a continent on the other side of the world, twelve hours and several latitudes away, where rains come without the spectacle of monsoon. She will search Google for grocery stores that sell fish that swim up tropical rivers from the sea every monsoon. She will drive forty miles to that store that sells frozen hilsa. And by sheer luck, she will find a frozen packet of hog plums on the veggie shelf. She will pay fifty dollars for the fish and a tip to get it cut and cleaned. She will ask her mother for the recipe over Skype, write it down with bullet points, and stick the recipe on the fridge with a souvenir magnet.

Once the ingredients are ready, she will set the non-stick pan on the electric burner, to recreate the taste her grandmother invented one rainy day.

ABOUT THE EDITORS

Mark Budman is a first-generation immigrant to the US. He is an engineer by training, but currently works as a medical interpreter. His fiction has appeared in *Catapult*, *Witness*, *World Literature Today*, *Mississippi Review*, *The London Magazine (UK)*, *McSweeney's*, *Painted Bride Quarterly*, and elsewhere. He is the author of the novel *My Life at First Try*, published by Counterpoint, and is the co-editor of anthologies published by Ooligan Press, Persea, Shanghai Foreign Language Education Press (China), and University of Chester (UK).

Budman loves to travel, so he can compare foreign countries to America, and appreciates the fine choice he made thirty-eight years ago when he came here. Learn more at markbudman.com.

Susan O'Neill is the author of two books: the fiction collection *Don't Mean Nothing* (Ballantine Books, UMass Press, and Serving House Books), and a slim volume of mostly humorous short essays, *Calling New Delhi for Free* (Peace Corps Writers Books). She co-edited *Vestal Review*, the oldest continuously running journal for flash fiction, from its beginnings in 2000 until 2020, and has published stories and essays in a fair number of literary magazines, virtual and print. She was nominated for the Pushcart twice, in fiction and in nonfiction, and once had a piece listed as a "Notable Essay" in *Best American Essays*.

O'Neill is also an RN and has a BA in Journalism. Indiana born and raised, she's lost count of the number of places she's lived, but they include a stint in the Army, most of which was spent working in an operating room in Vietnam, and a year in the Peace Corps in Venezuela, as well as shuffling around various locations in Massachusetts and Maine. She's worked in hospitals, nursing homes, and for a few years as an instructor in a nursing lab, and has been a reporter for weekly newspapers, a PR flak in a public library, and a lounge singer. She now lives in Brooklyn with her husband Paul, whom she met in Vietnam fifty years ago, and writes, edits, and mentors aspiring authors as a freelancer. Her website and essay blog can be found at susanoneill.us.

ABOUT THE AUTHORS

Elison Alcovendaz's work has appeared in *The Rumpus*, *Gargoyle Magazine*, *The Portland Review*, *Psychology Today Online*, and other publications. He has an MA in Creative Writing from Sacramento State, and once thought he'd be the first Filipino in the NBA.

Nancy Au is a second-generation Chinese-American immigrant. Her writing appears in *Vestal Review*, *Redivider*, *Gulf Coast*, *Michigan Quarterly Review*, *The Cincinnati Review*, *Catapult*, *Lunch Ticket*, *The Pinch*, and *SmokeLong Quarterly*, among others. Her flash fiction is included in the *Best Small Fictions 2018* anthology, and her writing was named Best Short Fiction of 2018 by *Entropy*. She was the winner of *Vestal Review*'s 2018 VERA Flash Fiction Prize, as well as the 2018 winner of *Redivider*'s Blurred Genre Contest. Her debut full-length collection, *Spider Love Song & Other Stories*, was a finalist for the 2020 CLMP Book Award for Fiction and listed among *Entropy Magazine*'s Best Fiction of 2019.

Genia Blum is a Swiss Ukrainian Canadian dancer, writer and translator, a second-generation immigrant to Canada, and a first-generation immigrant to Switzerland. Her work has been anthologized and published widely in literary journals, and she has received numerous Pushcart Prize and Best of the Net nominations. "Slaves of Dance," based on excerpts from her memoir in progress, was named a "Notable" in The *Best American Essays 2019*. Find @geniablum on Twitter and Instagram, or visit her website: www.geniablum.com. An earlier version of "The Ravine" was published in Lost Balloon in 2021.

Aida Bode is a poet and writer from former communist Albania. Her works have been published in a variety of online and print magazines, including *Silver Birch Press*, *Prelude*, *34th Parallel*, *Transcendent Zero Press*, *West Texas Literary Review*, *Three Line Poetry*, *The Raven's Perch*, as well as Albanian presses. She's also authored/translated the novel *David and Bathsheba*, two poetry volumes entitled *Rated* and *True Cheese*, and a quotes collection, *A Commuter's Eye View*. Aida holds an MA in English and Creative Writing. In 2017, Aida was selected as a Pushcart Nominee by *West Texas Literary Review*.

Raffi Boyadjian emigrated from Frankfurt, Germany, as a young child. He lives in Los Angeles with his wife and daughter. He's a graphic designer by trade, a composer by heart, and a confounding writer.

Philip Charter is a British writer who lives and works abroad. He teaches refugees and displaced people and is currently in Hong Kong. His work has been featured in numerous magazines and anthologies, such as *Storgy*, *Fictive Dream*, and *The National Flash Fiction Day* anthology. *Foreign Voices*, his debut collection, was published in 2018.

James Corpora's father, Calogero a.k.a. Alex, was born in Sicily and immigrated to this country at age five with his family; he grew up in Rockford, Illinois, and joined the Navy at age sixteen, using the birth certificate of an older brother.

Alex moved to California as a young man, and eventually went into business for himself. His son Jim was born and raised in L.A. and earned a BA in Economics at UCLA. He has published fiction in *The Paris Review* and other literary magazines and is a past recipient of a Fellowship in Literature from the National Endowment for the Arts. He has also been a writing fellow at Yaddo, the MacDowell Colony, and the Virginia Center for the Creative Arts.

Walerian Domanski was born in 1943. He lived in Poland, where he earned an MS degree in structural engineering. In 1980, he joined "The Solidarity" political and union movement and was a delegate for its 1981 National Convention. He was jailed in December 1981 by the regime of General Jaruzelski and immigrated to the USA five years later; there, he earned an MS in geotechnical engineering. He was known in Poland and now, around the world, as an editorial cartoonist, and in 2008, he began writing short stories. One of his stories, "Smoke factories," was published by the International PEN Club in London, England, in *The Magazine* in its fall 2010 edition.

Ingrid Jendrzejewski is a first-generation immigrant to the United Kingdom from the US. She serves as co-director of National Flash Fiction Day, Editor-in-Chief of *FlashBack Fiction* and *Flash Flood*, and is a flash editor at *JMWW*. Links to some of Ingrid's work can be found at www.ingridj.com, and she's on Twitter as @LunchOnTuesday. The story in *Short, Vigorous Roots* was first published in the *Los Angeles Review* in 2015.

Varya Kartishai is a first-generation American, a native Philadelphian whose parents were born in Ukraine. Her grandmother, who was herself illiterate, encouraged her to write. She has published short stories and poems in *Bewildering Stories* and *Page Bacon*, among others.

Masha Kisel is a first-generation immigrant from Ukraine to the United States. She has written personal essays on immigration and the Soviet experience for *The Forward*, *Times of Israel*, and the *Dayton Jewish Observer*. She holds a PhD in Slavic Languages and Literatures and currently teaches English at the University of Dayton.

Ruth Knafo Setton was born in Morocco and is the author of the novel *The Road to Fez*. She is the recipient of fellowships and awards from the National Endowment of the Arts, Pennsylvania Council on the Arts, *PEN*, *Writer's Digest*, *The Saturday Evening Post*, *Cutthroat*, and *Nimrod*. Her poetry, fiction, and creative nonfiction have been nominated for Pushcart Prizes and have appeared in many journals and anthologies, including *Tiferet*, *The North American Review*, *The Jerusalem Post*, *The Literary Traveler*, *Arts & Letters*, *Women Writing Desire*, *Becoming Myself: Reflections on Growing Up Female*, and *Best Contemporary Jewish Writing*. Her first screenplay was a finalist in numerous screenwriting competitions, including the Sundance Screenwriters' Lab. A former fiction editor of *Arts & Letters*, she has taught creative writing at Lehigh University and on Semester at Sea and is presently working on a new novel and a screenplay. She loves to travel in search of the myths and gods that connect us all.

Nina Kossman, an immigrant from Russia, is a bilingual writer, poet, and painter. Among her published works are two books of poems in Russian and English, two volumes of translations of Tsvetaeva's poems, a book of original poems in English, two books of short stories, an anthology published by Oxford University Press, and a novel. Her work has been translated into Greek, Japanese, Russian, and Spanish. She received a UNESCO/PEN Short Story Award, an NEA translation fellowship, and grants from the Foundation for Hellenic Culture, the Onassis Public Benefit Foundation, and Fundación Valparaíso. She lives in New York.

Rimma Kranet is a Russian-American fiction writer who emigrated with her family to the United States from Kiev (at the time, part of the ex-Soviet Union) to seek asylum from persecution and antisemitism. She has a Bachelor's Degree in English from the University of California Los Angeles. Her fiction has appeared in *Brilliant Flash Fiction*, *Construction Magazine*, *Club Plum*, and is forthcoming in *Coal Hill Review* and *Change Seven Magazine*. She splits her time between Florence, Italy, and Los Angeles, California.

Shaun Levin is a first-generation immigrant to Spain, previously to England, and before that to Israel, from South Africa. His books include *Seven Sweet Things*, *A Year of Two Summers*, and *Snapshots of The Boy*. He teaches creative writing and makes Writing Maps. See more at shaunlevin.com.

Amit Majmudar is a second-generation immigrant to the USA. He is the former first Poet Laureate of Ohio, and an internationally published poet and novelist.

Maija Mäkinen is a bilingual, Finnish-born writer with an MFA in Fiction from Boston University. Her stories have recently appeared in journals such as *Porter House*

Review (Pushcart nomination for short story), *The Bare Life Review*, and *SAND* Journal. The first chapter of her novel-in-progress received the University of Cambridge Lucy Cavendish Fiction Prize.

Sayantika Mandal is an Indian writer. She completed her MFA in Writing (Fiction) from the University of San Francisco, where she was awarded the Jan Zivic Fellowship, and is about to begin her PhD in English with a Creative Dissertation from the University of Georgia, Athens. Her writing has appeared in *The Citron Review*, *Dukool Magazine*, *Cerebration*, *Feminism in India*, *Times of India (Spellbound edition)*, and others. She is currently working on her first novel, with the working title *Driftwood*.

Erick Messias was born and raised in Brazil, where he completed medical school. He finished his residency in Baltimore, training in psychiatry and preventive medicine. He's now the Associate Dean for Faculty Affairs at the University of Arkansas for Medical Sciences College of Medicine, in Little Rock.

A. Molotkov was born in Russia and moved to the US in 1990 and switched to writing in English in 1993. His poetry collections are *The Catalog of Broken Things*, *Application of Shadows*, and *Synonyms for Silence*. His work has been published by *Kenyon Review*, *Iowa Review*, *Antioch Review*, *Massachusetts Review*, *Atlanta Review*, *Bennington Review*, and *Tampa Review*, *Hotel Amerika*, *Volt*, *Arts & Letters*, and many more. Molotkov has received various fiction and poetry awards and an Oregon Literary Fellowship. His translation of an Anton Chekhov story was included by Knopf in their Everyman Series, and his prose is represented by Laura

Strachan at Strachan Lit. He co-edits *The Inflectionist Review*. Please visit him at AMolotkov.com.

Feliz Moreno is a second-generation immigrant to the United States. She was born and raised in California and comes from a family of Mexican-American farm workers. She earned her MFA in Creative Writing at the University of San Francisco. She is currently working on a collection of short stories. Her writing has appeared or is forthcoming in *sPARKLE + bLINK*, *The Acentos Review*, *Longreads*, and *Apogee Journal*.

Kathy Nguyen is a Multicultural Women's and Gender Studies doctoral candidate at Texas Woman's University. Her parents became refugees after the fall of Sài Gòn in 1975, and permanently settled in Arkansas after temporarily being rehomed in Fort Chaffee's refugee camp. Her work has appeared in *Kartika Review*, *FIVE:2:ONE*, *diaCRITICS*, *Fearsome Critters*, and elsewhere. She is also a fiction and creative nonfiction reader at *CRAFT*. She learned to non-fluently read and write Vietnamese by watching Vietnamese karaoke DVDs, something her parents are bemused by.

Alexandros Plasatis is an immigrant ethnographer who writes fiction in English, his second language. His work has appeared in US, UK, Canadian, and Indian magazines and anthologies. He lives in the UK and works with asylum seekers. See more at alexandrosplasatis.com

Irina Popescu is a first-generation immigrant to the United States (from Romania). She is a mama, a writer, and a visiting professor of Latin American Studies at a small liberal arts college. She continues edging on the borders of identity, finding her life split between being "American" and "Romanian," whatever those two things mean.

Stuart Stromin is a South African-born writer and filmmaker. He immigrated to the United States and is living in Los Angeles. He was educated at Rhodes University, South Africa, the Alliance Francaise de Paris, and UCLA. His work has appeared in The Immigrant Report, Dissident Voices, Sheila-na-gig online, Alternating Current, Rigorous, Blood Puddles, among others.

Edvin Subašić was born and raised in Bosnia-Herzegovina. He left Bosnia in 1993, lived in a refugee camp in Croatia, and later in Germany. He immigrated to the US in 1997 at the age of 21 and learned English. He is the recipient of the 2018 Redivider Beacon Street Prize in Fiction and is in the MFA program at Boise State University. His work has been published in *McSweeney's Quarterly Concern*, *The Florida Review: Aquifer*, *Redivider*, *B O D Y Literature* in Prague, *Out-of-Stock*, and *The Cabin's "Writers in the Attic"* anthologies. He teaches English as a Second Language at Boise State University.

Yong Takahashi is the author of *The Escape to Candyland*. She won the Chattahoochee Valley Writers National Short Story Contest, and the *Writer's Digest*'s Write It Your Way Contest. She was a finalist in The Restless Books Prize for New Immigrant Writing, Southern Fried Karma Novel Contest, *Gemini Magazine* Short Story Contest, and Georgia Writers Association Flash Fiction Contest. She was awarded Best Pitch at the Atlanta Writers Club Conference.

Alizah Teitelbaum is a first-generation immigrant from the United States to Israel. Her stories and articles have appeared mostly in Jewish publications, but also in a secular anthology and a science fiction/fantasy magazine. One story, "Last Bus to Jerusalem," won first prize at the 2004 Moondance festival.

Lazar Trubman, a college professor from Moldavia, one of the republics that comprised the former USSR, immigrated to the United States in 1990, after surviving four years as a political prisoner in a Strict-Regime Colony in Northern Russia. His prose and poetry have appeared in *The Sea Letter, Forge Magazine, Bending Genres, Lit Mag, New Letters, Pithead Chapel, Here Comes Everyone, Selcouth Station Press, Passager Books*, and elsewhere.

Jose Varghese is a writer and translator from India, who has been living in Saudi Arabia since 2013 and teaches English in Jazan University. He edits two international literary journals and is working on his first novel. He is the author of *Silver Painted Gandhi and Other Poems*, and his short story "In/Sane" was a finalist for the Beverly Prize. His second poetry collection will be published by The Black Spring Press Group, in the UK, in 2021. He was a 2020 finalist for the London Independent Story Prize; a runner up for the Salt Flash Fiction Prize in 2013; and was shortlisted for the Retreat West Micro Fiction Competition in 2020. His works are published in *The Best Asian Short Story Anthology, Dreich Magazine, Meridian: The APWT Drunken Boat Anthology of New Writing, Step Outside the Frame: The APWT Special Edition, Borderless Journal, Bengaluru Review, Unthology 5, Unveiled, Reflex Fiction*, and *Flash Fiction Magazine.*

Marina Villa is a first-generation Cuban immigrant to the United States. She is the author of *Leaving Castro's Cuba: The Story of an Immigrant Family.*

Yara Zgheib is a traveler, reader, and writer. She was born in Beirut and has not stopped moving since (nor does she plan to). She is, in Michael Ondaatje's perfect words, "a mongrel of place. Of race. Of cultures. Of many genres." She knows what it means to belong nowhere and everywhere, and she believes there is freedom in that.